Alice and the Time Machine

Alice and the Time Machine

A Tale inspired by Lewis Carroll's Wonderland
and H. G. Wells' *The Time Machine*

by Victor Fet

ILLUSTRATED BY

BYRON W. SEWELL

evertype
2016

Published by Evertype, 73 Woodgrove, Portlaoise, R32 ENP6, Ireland. *www.evertype.com.*

This edition © 2016 Michael Everson.
Text © 2016 Victor Fet.
Illustrations © 2016 Byron W. Sewell.
Foreword © 2016 August A. Imholtz, Jr.

Advisory editor: Byron W. Sewell

Victor Fet has asserted his right under the Copyright, Designs and Patents Act, 1988, to be identified as the author of this work.

A catalogue record for this book is available from the British Library.

ISBN-10 1-78201-156-0
ISBN-13 978-1-78201-156-9

Typeset in De Vinne Text, Mona Lisa, ENGRAVERS' ROMAN, and *Liberty* by Michael Everson.

Illustrations: Byron W. Sewell.

Cover: Michael Everson.

Printed by LightningSource.

Foreword

*I*n one of the most often quoted passages from his religious and philosophical autobiography, the *Confessiones* written almost 1700 years ago, Saint Augustine says of the nature of time:

> Quid est ergo tempus? Si nemo ex me quaerat, scio; si quaerenti explicare uelim, nescio.

> 'What, then, is time? If no one ask of me, I know; if I wish to explain to him who asks, I know not.' (XI.14)

And yet Augustine then proceeds in the remaining 18 chapters of Book XI to demonstrate at some length that time itself does not exist because the past is no longer and the future is yet to be. Even the present has neither space nor duration—the present moment immediately becomes the past when we contemplate it. And yet, since we talk about time, Augustine next asks whether time exists only in the present—through memory of the past and prediction of the future. Finally, he inclines toward the conclusion that time must be a "distention" or "protraction of the mind". He analyses, again at some length, what happens when he recites from memory a psalm and what we must mean by "time".

> Ita carmen, ita pes, ita syllaba. Inde mihi uisum est nihil esse aliud tempus quam distentionem; sed cuius rei, nescio, et mirum, si non ipsius animi.

> 'And so for a poem, thus for a foot, thus for a syllable. Whence it appeared to me that time is nothing else than protraction; but of what I know not. It is wonderful to me, if it be not of the mind itself.' (XI.26)

In the end, he sees the mind "stretched out into temporality, into an apparent successiveness of events." This idea of the successiveness will have some echoes later.

Now no one, not even his harshest critics—and there have been and continue to be many, would accuse Augustine of writing science fiction, not even in his *De Civitate Dei,* but his conception of the distension or stretching of the mind may provide a way of looking not only at time but also at time travel, which even if it does not necessarily involve the mind or soul, is itself a central theme in the context of the genre of science fiction.

Let's then proceed with the idea of time travel itself, which is one of the main conceits of the present book by Victor Fet. It first may be worth noting a few classic historical examples of that "travel". Some science fiction literary scholars claim that time travel in the tradition of Indo-European literature may date back to the story of Kakudmi's daughter Revati, a girl of surpassing beauty, in the Hindu epic the *Mahābhārata* of more than two millennia ago. Revati and her father journey to the court of Krishna's brother, Lord Brahma himself, to find out who would be suitable to marry her. While Brahma listens to the music being played by the

Gandharvas—the gods' musicians and singers—they wait silently until Brahma speaks to them, whereupon they learn that 107 ages of man have passed since they arrived and all their friends and possible suitors are long dead. The story ends happily, a fact that is not always the case in time travel narratives, and Revati is promised in marriage to Vishnu, who is sojourning on earth in the form of Krishna.

Of course there are many other examples of fictional characters venturing out of time, usually into the past, from Odysseus in the *Odyssey* to Vergil's adaptation of that motif in the sixth book of the *Aeneid*, down to Dante's *Divine Comedy*. Poor Rip Van Winkle snoozes through time and even Alice herself, it might be argued, escapes into Wonderland time (for example, think of Time in the Mad Tea-Party) and Looking-Glass-land time (remember for example the White Queen who lives backwards!).

At an even more fanciful extreme of fictional time travel, the early 19th century Russian author Alexander Fomich Veltman wrote in 1836 the novel *Predki Kalimerosa* ('*The Ancestors of Kalimeros*'), in which the narrator travels back to fourth century BCE via a *hippogryph*, no less, a sort of animate time machine of great horse power, in the hope of finding out what made the ancient Greeks such great leaders—a recurrent Russian desire. The narrator arrives at the camp of Philip of Macedon (the father of Alexander the Great), meets Aristotle, and has several other adventures before concluding "that people of all times and places are the same, and it is the laws of history that can turn them into heroes."

A more modern narrative of time travel in reverse can be found in the 1983 *Alice Lengter Tilbake* ('*Alice Longs to Go Back*'), by Norwegian science fiction innovator Tor Åge Bringsværd. In this fairy tale, Alice, now an elderly woman, longs to return to the magic of Wonderland. Guided by two children, herself having been rejuvenated, she finds her way back to Wonderland and sees her old friends, including the White Rabbit, now sporting a very long beard; but she discovers to her dismay that it is now the Land of No-No, where fairy tales are forbidden!

Precisely a hundred years before the appearance of Brings-værd's book, however, the Oxford philosopher and logician, Francis Herbert Bradley, in his 1883 *Principles of Logic* described time in a way somewhat like Augustine's successiveness:

> We seem to think that we sit in a boat, and are carried down the stream of time, and that on the bank there is a row of houses with numbers on the doors. And we get out of the boat, and knock at the door of number 19, and, re-entering the boat, then suddenly find ourselves opposite 20, and having then done the same, we go on to 21. And, all this while, the firm fixed row of the past and the future stretches in a block behind us, and before us.

The idea of time as a stream of course can also be found in Isaac Watts' paraphrase of Psalm 90 "Our God, Our Help in Ages Past" published in 1719 in his book *The Psalms of David Imitated in the Language of the New Testament*. The antepenultimate stanza of his Psalm 90 reads:

> *Time, like an ever rolling stream,*
> *Bears all its sons away;*
> *They fly, forgotten, as a dream*
> *Dies at the opening day.*

The twentieth-century French philosopher Henri Bergson joined the succession of thinkers who considered the problem of "time", which for his part he understood as a construct of subjective experience. "A newborn baby," according to Bergson in his *Time and Free Will*, "would not experience time directly; he would have to learn how to experience it."

In 1895 the greatest science fiction novel of time travel to date appeared—*The Time Machine* by H. G. Wells, and set a standard for the idea of time travel that would last, as you can see, more than a century. Like *Alice's Adventures in Wonderland*, it has never been out of print.

Wells does not tell the reader exactly what his time machine is:

> "Now, it is very remarkable that this is so extensively overlooked," continued the Time Traveller, with a slight accession of cheerfulness. "Really this is what is meant by the Fourth Dimension, though some people who talk about the Fourth Dimension do not know they mean it. It is only another way of looking at Time. THERE IS NO DIFFERENCE BETWEEN TIME AND ANY OF THE THREE DIMENSIONS OF SPACE EXCEPT THAT OUR CONSCIOUS-NESS MOVES ALONG."

And his description of his model time machine is not too detailed:

> The thing the Time Traveller held in his hand was a glittering metallic framework, scarcely larger than a small clock, and very delicately made. There was ivory in it, and some transparent crystalline substance.
>
> "Now I want you clearly to understand that this lever, being pressed over, sends the machine gliding into the future, and this other reverses the motion. This saddle represents the seat of a Time Traveller."

R. H. Hutton, literary editor of *The Spectator*, pointed out in his 13 July 1895 review of *The Time Machine* that:

> The story is based on that rather favorite speculation of modern metaphysicians which supposed *time* to be at once the most important of the conditions of organic evolution, and the most misleading of subjective illusions... and yet Time is so purely subjective a mode of thought, that a man of searching intellect is supposed to be able to devise the means of travelling in time as well as in space, and visiting, so as to be contemporary with, any age of the world or future, so as to become as it were a true "pilgrim of eternity."

And interestingly a letter published in *Nature* in 1885, and signed only with the single initial "S", had anticipatorily raised the idea of time as a fourth dimension:

> What is the fourth dimension?... I propose to consider Time as a fourth dimension... Since this fourth dimension cannot be introduced into space, as commonly understood, we require a new kind of space for its existence, which we may call time space.

Science fiction scholar Paul Kincaid observed of the time machine idea specifically that:

> The time machine allows not movement in time (we already live in time, and a novelist has always been able to set a story in any future or past), but transposition in time. It has introduced to science fiction the facility of anachronism, of looking at any one period through alien eyes. As such, it may be the most archetypal device in the genre.

And Roslynn Haynes commented on Wells' anticipation, as it were, of Einstein:

Apart from its powerful imagery *The Time Machine* is conceptually intriguing. Wells analyzes the idea of a time dimension, and once we accept the fantasy of travelling through time, he forestalls any philosophical objections. This is the more amazing when we consider that he originally wrote it seventeen years before publication of Albert Einstein's Theory of Special Relativity, the first scientific paper to address the concept of time as the fourth dimension. The descriptions of the machine's departure and arrival are wholly consistent with Einstein's illustration of the two clocks, one stationary and one moving.

Finally, Peter Nicholls claimed that "Wells in *The Time Machine* seems to have used the simplest of all models of time, in which it is seen as a river. The Time Traveller goes further and further downstream into the future." In 1900, the great novelist, and no mean critic, Henry James wrote to H. G. Wells to express his admiration for *The Time Machine* and said "You are very magnificent."

In Victor Fet's novel his time machine, which he calls "the Macchinetta"—not to be confused with a coffee machine of the same name, which had not been invented at the time in which he sets his he novel—is an improvement over the Wells' Time Machine in that it can transport/transpose two people rather than just one.

Victor Fet, the preeminent biologist, scorpion researcher, poet and translator, includes in this book more science than one usually finds in science fiction or other novels. He brings together, the well-travelled H. G. Wells himself, Charles

Darwin, Charles Lutwidge Dodgson* (that is, Lewis Carroll), John Dalton, and—*mirabile dictu*—Alice Pleasance Liddell—the Alice of *Alice's Adventures in Wonderland*!

In his seventy-second year, toward the end of his long life, Augustine wrote in his *Retractationes* (we might translate that title as "Reconsiderations") of his earlier *Confessiones* "What others think about these things is a matter for them to decide. Yet I know that they have given and continue to give pleasure to many." It is hoped that *Alice and the Time Machine* will give you as much pleasure reading it as Victor Fet had in writing it and his friends have had in reading it.

August A. Imholtz, Jr.
29 February 2016

---

* It is worth reminding the reader that Dodgson and his family pronounced the name [ˈdɒdsən] ("Dodson") and not [ˈdɒdʒsən] "Dodge-son").

Alice and the Time Machine

CONTENTS

CHAPTER I

Barnacles and a
Strange Visitor

In 1857, when Alice was five years old, her father, Christ Church's newly appointed Dean, Henry George Liddell, took her along with his beautiful young wife, Lorina, and their five children on a two-week's holiday to Llandudno. They had spent most of the holiday in one of the elegant seaside hotels where the children had frolicked in the surf along the beach, but on one occasion they had taken a side trip to Anglesey, where for the first time, Alice had discovered—firmly anchored to rocks, seashells, and the rotting timbers of an old shipwreck—what would, curiously, for such a young girl, become one of her greatest passions: the acorn barnacle, that hated and much maligned bane of many a sailing ship's owner and captain. Against her parents' protestations, she had finally managed to convince them to allow her to take a small basketful of oyster shells, each gaily festooned with barnacles, back to Oxford.

5

She had thought of little else once she had discovered these fascinating intertidal crustaceans. To Alice, fairy-tale gryphons and unicorns were not nearly as amazing than these strange filter-feeders who somehow managed to hitch rides and tour the vast oceans in style on large fish and flukes of whales. Her father had explained that England had become the world's fastest naval power once they had fitted her ships' hulls with copper to prevent barnacle fouling. Hearing this, she had sucked on a penny—a heavy, shiny coin on which one could read "VICTORIA DEI GRATIA" around her Majesty's profile—to find out what copper tasted like and agreed with the barnacles that copper's metallic taste was horrid and was to be avoided at all costs.

Alice's fondness for barnacles, and natural history collections she carefully amassed and studied in the summertime, inevitably brought her to the Oxford Museum of Natural History, which had opened in 1860. As a frequent and enthusiastic visitor she was allowed to visit the collections in backrooms where she helped curators to sort fascinating specimens collected from all the oceans. It was there that Alice was introduced to the greatest barnacle expert and the most famous naturalist in the world.

In 1866, when Alice first met Mr Charles Darwin, he was fifty-seven. Alice was familiar with his famous 1859 book, *On the Origin of Species*, which attempted to explain similarities of organisms as having descended from a common ancestor while later becoming quite unlike each other—as, say, a lobster and a barnacle! This seemed quite obvious to her, and she couldn't understand why the book caused so much controversy.

Since Mr Darwin was a gentleman-naturalist of independent means, he did not need to hold a university position in order to conduct his studies. His collections from the 1830s expedition on *HMS Beagle*, were conveniently kept in his spacious home in Down, Kent,[1] nicknamed Down House, where he and his family had lived since 1842. Being of poor health, Darwin no longer travelled on collecting expeditions.

Every visit to Down House, like the one today, found Alice drowning again and again in the bright well of a microscope.[2] How she wished that she could visit the exotic islands where young Darwin and other naturalists had collected these very specimens! The Guianas and the Antilles, Santo Domingo and Galápagos! Alice sighed, realizing that a 14-year-old girl could not possibly travel alone to foreign parts—even within the relative safety of the British Empire. There was simply no chance that her parents would consider taking her much further afield than Llandudno or the Riviera.

"Perhaps—" Alice thought, while she diligently filled in the Latin names on calligraphic labels for the glass jars containing barnacles, "—when I grow up I might marry a handsome and brilliant young explorer. A botanist, perhaps, and we can travel the globe together, working for the British Museum! He will collect exotic plants and I shall collect animals. We will be the perfect match! Wouldn't it be wonderful, if we could even own a small ship of our own? He would have to be very rich of course, like Mr Darwin. It would be so exciting! Our children could grow up aboard ship and help us collect! I shall teach them all I know about barnacles!"

Immersed in her romantic daydream, Alice hadn't noticed that Darwin had entered the study room. He coughed quietly and Alice turned to see who it was. "Oh! Mr Darwin! I didn't hear you come in!" She immediately stood up and curtsied to him and a companion, a younger, moustached man.

"I see that you are very busy, Alice!" Darwin remarked. "If you can spare a few minutes I would like to introduce a very special friend of mine."

"But of course!" Alice replied looking directly at Darwin's visitor.

"Alice, this is Mr Herbert Wells." He paused briefly and gestured to him. "Mr Wells, this is Alice Liddell, one of the daughters of Dean Henry George Liddell of Christ Church. You no doubt know that he is one of the co-authors of the Greek-English lexicon."

"Yes, an immense and invaluable work," said the guest. Alice extended her hand, which Wells took gently. "It's a pleasure to meet you, Alice. Mr Darwin has told me of your great enthusiasm for barnacles."

"And you," she replied with a warm smile. "It's true that I am quite fascinated by barnacles. There is such a marvellous variety. I only wish that someday I might find a barnacle that Mr Darwin hasn't already discovered, but I know the chance for that is extremely small."

"I wouldn't be at all surprised if you did just that!" Darwin said, before changing the subject. "Mr Wells is from the future," Darwin remarked, as calmly as he might have said that he was from Scotland.

Alice's eyebrows shot up at his remark. "I must have misunderstood what you just said—from the future? Surely you jest!"

Darwin smiled. "I used to believe in that apparent impossibility myself. It is certainly a strange thing to contemplate. Mr Wells has a time machine that allows him to travel backwards into the past."

Alice giggled. "That's very funny, Mr Darwin. It sounds like something Mr Dodgson might dream up in one of his fairy-tales."

"No, it's no fairy-tale! I'm quite serious. He has returned from the future to visit me."

Alice's expression changed to a serious one. "I know you would not lie to me, Mr Darwin," she said. "How far into the past can you travel, Mr Wells?"

"Not very far yet," Wells replied. "I'm still experimenting with it to see how far I can extend its range."

"Precisely how far have you come from on this trip?" asked Alice, now quite intrigued by such a crazy possibility.

"I've come from the year 1898."

Alice was naturally skeptical. "I would like to believe you, but how can you prove it? I fear that you are teasing me to see how gullible I might be!"

Wells thought for a moment and then reached into his pocket and retrieved a few coins. "Here, this penny is relatively new; minted just last year. You can see that the date is 1897." He handed it to Alice.

Alice looked very closely at the bronze penny, then back into Wells' penetrating blue eyes. "The date could have been a minting error—but this coin has a profile of an elderly woman! Who is she?"

Wells smiled. "That's how her Majesty Queen Victoria is depicted in my time. We celebrated a half-century of her reign in 1887." He studied the other coins in his hand. "Here's a 'jubilee' shilling from 1892." He handed it to her. "And here's a gold sovereign from 1872, still with the young Queen."

Alice studied the coins. "Well, I guess I have no choice except to believe you," she said. "Curiouser and curiouser! So you came from 1898—that would be thirty-two years from now! I will be an old lady by then!" she said.

"I don't think that you will really be all that old, but you will certainly be much older than me! My actual age is thirty-two." Wells laughed. "You see, on your timeline I wo'n't be born until next September; right now I am just an embryo residing in my mother's womb. She resides at 47 High Street in Bromley."

Alice thought for a moment. "That's just seven miles from here to the North."

"Yes, that's correct," Wells agreed. "You're very quick with your sums—and your maps!"

"I didn't know that time travel was possible!" said Alice, still quite amazed at what he had said, as well as at the coins, especially the penny.

"Neither did I," interrupted Darwin. "When Mr Wells appeared here at Down House last month with his outrageous story, it seemed like the ravings of a hatter. Nonetheless, here he is! Neither ghost nor spirit, but a person of flesh and blood. I know it's hard to believe that a person can visit us here from the future—even from such a near future as the 1890s. However, it didn't take him long to convince me."

"How did you convince Mr Darwin?" Alice asked Wells. "With a penny?"

"No, I took Mr Darwin for a ride on my time machine," Wells said through a broad smile. "Just a short one; only a few years; both ways up and down the Earth's current time-line."

Alice frowned. "That sounds very dangerous," she said. "You might get lost forever and never find your way back!"

"I understand why Mr Darwin is so fond of you! You are a very clever young girl! You're quite correct. One must be very careful."

Darwin interrupted again. "Time is an enigmatic fellow. I got into close acquaintance with him when I was studying rocks and fossils."

Alice's mind was suddenly racing with intriguing questions. "Tell me, Mr Wells, can you meet your previous or future self?"

"Yes, it's possible, but there isn't any real danger in such a meeting."

"Why is that?" she asked. "Isn't it possible that events might be changed by interference with the past?"

Mr Wells regarded her with even greater interest. "You are very bright indeed! That's a very good question. Yes, I suspect they can indeed be changed. One must be very careful."

"But how do you move in time?" she asked, her curiosity growing.

"Excuse me for just a minute," Wells said. "I need to retrieve something I left in the smoking room."

"Of course," Darwin said.

"A few moments later Wells returned to the study, carrying a heavy, strange-looking device.

"Is that a microscope?" Alice asked, studying it intently. "It looks rather scientific, what with the jumble of bronze and crystal blocks! Is that ivory? What are all of the knobs, levers, and lenses for? And why is it humming?"

"This, Alice, is my dear device. I think of it as a small time-ship. I christened her 'the Macchinetta', which is Italian for 'a small machine'. It functions quite well, but with limitations. For example, it can only transport two people—myself and a single passenger—within a range of approximately a hundred years into the past and then back to the future until I come up against my own time line, where it abruptly stops."

"Why ca'n't it take you further?"

"I don't know, though I think one possibility is that my personal future doesn't yet exist. The past, however, obviously already existed. For some reason that I don't yet understand, the Macchinetta comes to a halt in the past when I reach Napoleonic times and it absolutely refuses to go any further back. There are many things I don't yet know about it: how it works; what it uses for fuel; such things as that."

"Surely, you must know its energy source."

"No; I can only guess. I think one possibility might be some type of magnetism."

"But aren't you the one who built it?" she asked.

"Goodness, no!" exclaimed Wells. "Even with my Bachelor of Science degree from the University of London—in Zoology, mind you—I wouldn't remotely know how to design and build such things. I discovered this device quite by chance in an antiquities shop in the West End. The owner had died and the shop's stock had been placed for sale by his widow. I bought the Macchinetta for ten pounds. Its function was completely unknown to the widow, a rather coarse woman who was glad to be rid of it. I can only surmise that it's an artifact from another civilization—in our world or beyond it; perhaps a future civilization or one from another world that we know nothing about. The Macchinetta demonstrates that time travel is possible! Perhaps it's a gift to entice man to travel into the future or back into the past. Or perhaps it was tragically lost by some unknown time traveller."

Alice considered this and then observed, "Perhaps that time traveller is now lost in the past desperately searching for his time machine so that he can return to his life in some distant future, but now you have it and he ca'n't find it."

Wells shrugged. "There is no way to know. I certainly hope that such a tragedy is not my doing."

Darwin interjected himself into their conversation. "Surely this strange apparatus uses some sophisticated mathematics far beyond Euclid's."

"Mr Dodgson vehemently denies non-Euclidean geometry,"[3] Alice remarked.

"Mr Dodgson is an excellent mathematician and logician," Darwin acknowledged, "but all of the sciences advance and he may be wrong. Anyway, when Mr Wells first came here it was not by chance; he sought my help. He tells me that my book of 1859 created a great commotion within the next decades."

"It's one of the most influential books ever written," confirmed Wells. "And Mr Darwin is currently working on yet another—a book even more revolutionary!"

"What is it about," she asked; "if it's not a secret, of course?"

"It's not a secret! It's my theory about how man has evolved and changed, and will continue to evolve and change in the future. I was certainly shocked that a future man would come to me for that!" Darwin admitted. "Progress is synonymous with the future, as it must be. Think for a moment about the enormous technological advances man has already achieved! Why, Mr Wells tells me that someone in the near future has invented something called 'wireless'. He describes it as a telegraphic device, potentially superior to the Hughes machine! Can you imagine?"

"But why are you telling me all of this?" Alice demanded. "I am not a famous scholar or an inventor to be confided in, I do not know of these matters. I am just interested in barnacles."

"Not so," said Wells. "In my own time you have, in your own way, become as famous as Mr Darwin! The story of *Alice's Adventures in Wonderland* that Dodgson told you and your two sisters has sold thousands of copies in the past three decades! Practically everyone in England knows a quotation or two from the story. We would like to ask you about this very strange book."

Alice hesitated. "It *is* a strange story, isn't it? That is so sad! I wish that it had never been published!"

"Really? But why?!" exclaimed Wells and Darwin simultaneously. "What do you mean?"

"Well, you see," said Alice, "Mr Dodgson kindly took the responsibility of publishing this story under his name."

Wells did not quite understand. "He *is* the author, isn't he?"

"Not really," sighed Alice. "The story indeed sounds like a kind of nonsense that one might tell to little children—about elves and such; only there were no real elves and fairies in this one; that story was never told by Mr Dodgson to me and my sisters."

Now both Wells and Darwin were lost. "Why then does he say he authored it?" asked Darwin.

"To protect me," said Alice. She remembered now, and her eyes suddenly welled with tears. "On that day, the 4th of July 1862, I had a terrible vision. You will really need to ask Mr Dodgson about that—"

"Say no more," interrupted Darwin gently. "The issue is getting complicated, and I think that some first-hand explanations are due. Besides, I see your governess behind the glass doors closing her Miss Austen novel. It must be time for you to go back home for today.

"Let me write to Mr Dodgson and invite him to come from Oxford for dinner next Saturday—and both of you of course are welcome as well. I am sure we can have a fruitful conversation. Now, Wells," Darwin chuckled, "I am afraid that I wo'n't be able to send you a letter to confirm the invitation—the Royal Mail of 1866 does not deliver to 1898. Come anyway."

"The Royal Mail still goes strong in my time, all around the globe," assured Wells. "I truly hope it will continue to do so—a civilization without communication would not be efficient. Saturday it is, let me mark my 1866 calendar."

CHAPTER II

Alice's True Story

ollowing a sumptous meal of plaice and turtle soup, Alice, Charles Dodgson, H. G. Wells, and an elderly gentleman introduced as John Dalton joined Darwin in his study where they seated themselves in elegant high-backed Georgian wing-chairs arranged in front of his desk. The light from two oil lamps on the desk created a sense of coziness and comfort. Beautifully framed hand-coloured engravings of some of the specimens Darwin had collected on his early voyages of discovery hung on the papered walls. Opposite the desk hung a steel-engraving of *The Beagle* tossed precariously in a tempest on the edge of a typhoon, a stark reminder of the risks he had taken.

Wells had seated himself next to where his Macchinetta sat on the worn Persian carpet. The time machine's levers were in fail-safe, locked postions, and its crystals were dark.

Darwin, seated behind his desk, opened the discusion in a soft voice. "Thank you for coming this evening. I hope that dinner was acceptable."

Everyone nodded and Wells enthusiastically added, "Hear! Hear! Excellent, my good fellow!"

Darwin smiled, then spoke directly to Dodgson. "Thank you for providing Mr Wells and Mr Dalton copies of your famous *Alice*."

Dodgson acknowledged him with a slight nod. "Yes, I'm curious to hear what this august group has to say about it."

Darwin turned to Wells and Dalton. "I assume that you both carefully read the book." They nodded. "Good. On behalf of the three current members of the Time Club, I want to welcome new members Miss Alice Liddell and her friend, Mr Charles Dodgson. Tonight Mr Wells has brought Mr John Dalton from Manchester of 1832. He told me earlier this evening that he knew my grandfather quite well."

"What did you just say?" Dodgson asked, assuming he must have misunderstood. "From 1832?"

"Yes, 1832. Mr Wells travelled back in time and brought him here to meet with us tonight."

"Nonsense!" Dodgson declared.

"No, I'm quite serious! From 1832. Mr Wells has a time machine that allows him to travel back into the past and bring people forward into our present. That's what we are meeting about tonight."

Dodgson was understandably skeptical and turned to Dalton. "Do you claim to be *the* John Dalton? The person credited with having founded the atomic theory?"

Dalton nodded. "Yes. I realize that it's hard to believe."

Dodgson looked around at the group. "You're all mad! I don't want to go among mad people!" He stood up to leave.

"Wait!" Darwin said. "Please. We obviously need to convince you about time travel. What if Mr Wells were to take you back to Daresbury in the year 1837? You would be five or six I suppose. I believe that Daresbury was where you were born, am I correct?"

"Yes," Dodgson said. "I only wish that it was possible to do just that and that you weren't playing this elaborate charade at my expense!"

"If we did this, would you then be convinced?" asked Darwin.

"Of course, but that is quite impossible!"

Darwin turned to Wells. "Can you give him a quick trip to Daresbury on your machine?"

"Of course. We can simply latch onto his time line. We ca'n't miss it."

"How long until you can go and return? We don't have all night. Alice will need to go home in a few hours. Her governess will be getting anxious."

"Approximately twenty minutes should be long enough for a simple look around." Wells stood up and made a few adjustments to the machine next to his chair. The crystals slowly illuminated with a bluish light and there was now a faint, high-pitched humming noise emanating from somewhere inside the mysterious machine. "Come over here Mr Dodgson," Wells said, "and grab hold of that handle on the other side. Hold on tightly. Whatever happens, do not let go of your grip. We don't want to lose you out there somewhere in time!" Wells made a few adjustments to the dials and levers then asked Dodgson if he was ready. Dodgson, still skeptical, decided to humour him. "Yes." Two seconds later they suddenly and silently vanished. Darwin noted the time of their departure on his pocket watch.

Fifteen minutes later the Macchinetta and the time travellers appeared, suspended in the air, two feet above the floor. They slowly descended to the same spot where they stood before departure. Dodgson was in tears and sobbing uncontrollably.

Darwin rushed over to him and asked, "Are you in pain, Mr Dodgson? Have you been injured?"

Dodgson shook his head, unable to speak. Finally after a few minutes and some unintelligible stammering he managed to blurt out, "I—just saw my—self as a—a—a five-year old boy, playing with two of my sisters in a field near our old home in Daresbury! And then—" he continued gasping and with more sobbing, "—I saw my young mother! It was a sunny summer day! I could smell new-mown hay! What sort of spiritual or magical trick were you doing? Which fairies do you command?"

"Do you believe in fairies, Mr Dodgson?" Darwin asked.

"Why, yes, as a matter of fact, I do! Were fairies somehow involved?"

"No one here except you believes in fairies, magic or spiritualism." Darwin said. "We are scientists! You just took a travel back along your personal timeline to your youth."

Dodgson looked stunned. "Really?"

"Quite!" Darwin said. "We ca'n't make this happen! It is far away from our limited abilities and knowledge! Are you convinced now?"

Dodgson nodded. "That was the most astonishing thing I have ever experienced! Can I go back?"

"No! This is not a parlour entertainment like breathing nitrous oxide! This is very serious inquiry. We want your help, but we don't have time to play games with you."

Dodgson's head was still swimming as he turned to John Dalton: "So it *is* true—you are *the* famous Mr Dalton of the atomic theory fame? Sir, I know little of chemistry—I just use quite a bit of its practical side in my photography—but I am deeply awed by numerical permutations that you and others developed, of tiny invisible particles of nature, the atoms making up larger molecules."

The word "atom" was familiar to Alice from her Greek history lessons. She wondered if Dalton's atoms were the same as those of Democritus and Parmenides, but was not sure she was not confusing the names. Alice also recalled that Plato did not like atoms—he maintained that atoms just crashing into other atoms would never produce all the beauty of the world. She thought Mr Dodgson rather resembled a young Plato, and tried to imagine him on the Agora below the Parthenon as a faithful pupil of a bearded Socrates— who would rather resemble Mr Darwin.

"A very clever system indeed," continued Dodgson with agitation, "and, if true, the old Pythagoras himself would be elated. I wish he were here to see how modern science employs his numerical magic rules, the music of spheres akin to the Cabbalism—"

Darwin turned to Wells. "What does your future science tell us of those number games? I know that John Newlands of the Royal College of Chemistry just postulated a Law of Octaves in describing atoms as he would music, in a very Pythagorean way. Strange! Does Dalton's theory still hold up in the 1890s or was Newlands correct?"

"Dalton's theory is well accepted," said Wells. "Moreover, Newlands was ridiculed in your time, but his contribution has since been recognized—after the Germans and the Russians produced similar results. There is a Russian chemist who offered a 'Periodic Table of Elements'. All their qualities are explained by chess-like positions in rows and columns. More importantly, the Russian—whose name evades me at the moment—claimed that he saw his Table in a dream, where all the chemical elements fell into place as required."

"As in a perfect puzzle!" smiled Dodgson. "I do believe that there is such a thing as numerical magic; some of our parlour games are more than just games, you know! The harmony of nature—or at least the part of it that we can comprehend— ought to be built on simple numbers and their combinations. I might be a bit old-fashioned, but one should give the eighteenth century some credit for elucidating simple rules of nature!"

"Don't idealize our time," Dalton sadly replied. "It had its temptations and we did not pass some of its trials. I don't want to sound too didactic, but it would be unwise for your generations to repeat our mistakes."

"Excuse me, gentlemen, but can we get back to our planned discussion?" Darwin asked, trying to keep the discussion from wandering off and down rabbit-holes. He turned to Alice. "Alice, would you like to be excused while we discuss your intriguing case? From what Mr Dodgson wrote in reply to my invitation, I expect it might be unpleasant for you to relive again the perturbances you experienced that July afternoon in 1862. We could spare you the ordeal."

"No," Alice answered. "I'd like to stay and hear what you have to say. I'm eager to know what people will think when the secret is out. I'm actually rather relieved to be getting it out in the open. Mr Wells tells us that the whole world thirty years from now is enchanted with this silly tale of Wonderland! I ca'n't understand why anyone would find it amusing."

"I don't mean to offend you, Mr Dodgson," Dalton said, "but I will speak bluntly. I find it distressing and hard to comprehend that in future decades civilized people will actually be amused with such unbelievable nonsense as fills your *Alice* book! I didn't find any of your weird word jokes the least bit amusing—rather, it's a nightmarish, childish fantasy!"

"It *is* a kind of nonsense," admitted Dodgson mildly, determined not to get offended or caught up in an argument with Dalton, "but it is nonsense derived from a lack of logic or its misuse; logical nonsense, if you will. Even children can see the problems that it creates and laugh at its jokes or implications. Honestly, I am quite surprised by the almost immediate popularity of *Alice's Adventures in Wonderland*—why, there is a rumour that even Queen Victoria herself has read and enjoyed my tale! I suggest that this kind of nonsense is entertaining because it violates apparently logical rules of our reality and our language."

"Your present society pays too much attention to all sorts of games and entertainments," replied Dalton. "I have nothing against good relaxation; a sport of hunting or a passion for gardening—but seeing adult, educated Englishmen involved in incessant parlour games, charades and the theatre is utterly childish! And so many of those new implements that you scientists have recently invented are used primarily to kill time, not to save it! Mr Wells tells me that moving pictures have been invented in his decade—by the French, no doubt! It's not hard to imagine that soon no one will read or write anymore, but rather just sit and watch moving *Punch* cartoons. Like your dear barnacles, Alice: a society of sessile filter-feeders. Consider this bizarre thing written in the *Alice* book, where it says, '*it is always tea-time, and and we've no time to wash the things between whiles.*' Is this the shape of things to come? Stuff and nonsense!"

"So let us return to this book!" said Darwin. "Everyone knows it as Mr Dodgson's clever, comic fantasy for children. The book employs traditional literary device of a dream, which even the Bard himself employed generously—with *The Midsummer Night's* adventures and all that. However, now we are told that *Alice's Adventures in Wonderland* was *not* Mr Dodgson's literary fantasy disguised as child's dream. Please, Mr Dodgson, tell us about it."

Dodgson sighed and took out a large leather-bound notebook. "I thank you all, gentlemen, for inviting me and Miss Liddell here today and for your trust and confidence. I appreciate this opportunity to disclose, after four years of uneasiness, my evidence of this strangest episode of my life.

On the 4th of July 1862, during a boating trip on the Isis, we had a picnic on the river bank. It rained—a small, sudden shower, and we took shelter. At that time, Alice experienced a vivid vision, as she clearly recited what she saw with her mind's eye. She was lying on the grassy bank, with her head in the lap of her sister. She was not aware of what was happening—but started talking incessantly, slowly, in a very even voice, as if reciting a stage part.

"It is quite interesting that no one—neither myself, nor Alice's sisters, nor my friend Robinson Duckworth who accompanied us—was frightened at this point or tried to stop her. Nobody panicked; no one ran for help. It was as if Alice was reciting her memorized school lesson.

"Everyone recalls being strangely enchanted and pacified by a torrent of intense and weird imagery rapidly coming towards them—a rabbit-hole descent, a magic garden, body size changes, a sea of tears, giant mushrooms, and blue caterpillars—all this bright, unmistakably childish, nursery-style nonsense. I immediately started taking down Alice's utterances in a form of shorthand, in which I have a reasonable skill, and managed to fill this thick notebook I brought to show you today.

"My original transcript of this incredible event begins in the middle of a sentence that reads: '*a White Rabbit with pink eyes just ran close to me. There is nothing so very remarkable in that*'.

"Alice talked—dictated, in fact—without stopping for almost three hours. Finally, she uttered the words '*You're nothing but a pack of cards!*' Then she immediately came to. She gave a little scream, half of fright and half of anger, and then sat up and said: 'Oh, I've had such a curious dream!' She nearly lost her voice, and was given tea to sooth her dry mouth and throat.

"Everyone by that time was hot, hungry, thirsty, and tired (we couldn't possibly have our tea while Alice was talking). Alice herself did not remember much of her vision. Even today the book seems very foreign and rather boring to her. She avoids re-reading it, and tells me that she was never at the slightest amused by its quaint nonsense as most other people are—and will be for a long time, as Mr Wells tells us.

"This is the truth, and it was a secret that we tried to keep private for obvious reasons." Dodgson sighed and looked at the others. "I'd like to hear your opinion now."

"A perfectly natural explanation of this phenomenon is possible," said Darwin, who had remained rather quiet until that moment. "Alice's transformations—changes in her size, in lengths of her neck and legs—are well-known in medical literature as *metamorphopsia*.[4] This condition could be due to an infection or a headache; or even food poisoning. And certainly, similar hallucinatory effects of mushrooms are well known, when eaten or inhaled.[5] That is what drove the fierce Vikings to madness."

"But I was not ill!" protested Alice. "I did not have a headache; and I most definitely did not eat—or inhale—any mushrooms! We had our picnic baskets stuffed with perfectly regular items; nothing out of the ordinary. Miss Prickett would not let us consume any imperfect food!"

"The day was hot, and you felt very sleepy," reminded Darwin. "Temperature changes alone are known to produce deep mental effects, playing tricks with blood pressure and heartbeat. I am not a medical doctor, but I spent two years in Edinburgh studying medicine in my youth. I have recorded many strange cases in my travels among sailors—and among the natives. I also collected information on human emotions and have a huge card index of abnormal manifestations, like this one: A sensation of your rabbit-hole descent, which takes four pages in print. Its characteristic refrain was (he consulted the book's Chapter I): *'Down, down, down'* ... *'four thousand miles down ... I shall fall right through the earth!'*

"While I do not completely exclude the chemical effect of certain substances in your food or drink, those are not even necessary. A human body could be easily convinced into experiencing hallucinations. Shamanistic practices in South America—which I witnessed first-hand in my youth—routinely involve what we classify as hypnotism."

"I doubt that possibility," said Dalton. "We see no possible source of a hypnotist, like a shaman or a Druid, present anywhere near Alice on that day."

"Now," said Wells, "we come to the most interesting point." He looked up from his notes. "You would excuse me, Alice—but, before we started our meeting, Mr Dodgson told me that, on that day, as you fell into a deep, medium-like trance, he was sure that you were in contact with some kind of a fairy world. As you heard him say earlier, he believes in fairies."

Alice smiled. "I know," she said, "Mr Dodgson does believe in pixies. But then many adults do. They also get upset when children tell them it is all fantasy. So we try not to disillusion them. Children stop believing in St Nick years before the adults find the nerve to tell them that he is a fictional character—so we keep pretending we believe in him while we don't."

Everyone turned to Dodgson, who tried to defend his position, stuttering: "M–m–many educated and respected men believe firmly that the supernatural world exists. Instances of mediumism abound and are amply documented—by Monsieur Kardec in France, a well-known educator; and that famous American medium who came to London over a decade ago. Mesmerism is an accepted part of science. Our understanding of such worlds is nil or close to nil.

"What we think or believe about elves and fairies and leprechauns, might be, partly, true: manifestations of the supernatural as seen through the senses of humans, taking traditional folkloric forms. Alice could have experienced the same type of vision as the bards such as Thomas the Rhymer used to have—the contacts as such are undoubtedly reflected in humanity's recorded poetry."

"Do you, sir, dismiss human imagination entirely?" inquired Dalton indignantly. "Are we to believe in the Celtic wood sprites—or, like savages of the Oceania, that the *mana* of our ancestors sustains our life—or to behave like the superstitious Greeks for whom every spring contained a pretty nymph, and every meadow a goat-legged faun? I thought that by the 1860s England would have gone a long way to shed such naïve, uncivilized beliefs. Please leave that to your fanciful literature for little children!"

"I do not deny imaginative powers to human beings; quite the opposite!" replied Dodgson. "What I am saying is that stories and fairy-tales, as Plato's ideas, could exist in a 'parallel world'—those mysterious Avalons, which touch our reality and intersect with it as three-dimensional geometric figures. Widespread beliefs in the supernatural must be based upon something existing in some kind of reality.

"Please look at the collective spiritual labour of many generations, legends and songs sung for so long in certain sensitive places of nature—how could all that just vanish without any trace? Akin to prayers, they might belong to a more refined matter, composition of which is not yet clear to us. Even in Spiritualist séances we do not truly know what is happening, so capricious are the conditions of every case.

"I know that my Church does not approve of such views. The Roman Catholics even put a prohibition in their Catechism—something about divination and talking with ghosts. I am a man of the cloth—but exactly because of that,

I should not easily dismiss the world of miracles and belief. After all, we have the Revelation; and the Hebrews had their prophets inspired divinely; and the Virgin has been seen in our time, although many doubt this. Why ca'n't there be a place for the worlds beyond our perception, but ruled by Providence?"

His frantic words hung in the air as the others found immediate objections to most of what he had said. Wells smoked calmly. Dalton shrugged and turned to his copy of Dodgson's book.

Alice found it hard to concentrate. Her head was slightly spinning from the intensity of the conversation—and the tobacco smoke. The meeting suddenly turned into a very serious dispute, far more so than any light table-talk she had ever have heard from the adults who come together on summer days.

"Fresh air!" called Darwin, and playfully grabbed a small bronze bell from a shelf, which he rang as a schoolmaster would. "We need a break and some nourishment. The tea is served outside on the lawn, with scones and clotted cream— and, for the grown-ups, some drops of a more serious drink, whether they believe in pixies or not. We will return in an hour to resume; no serious talk until then."

Mr Dalton's Eyeballs

*F*eeling refreshed, the members of the Time Club returned to Darwin's study. Speaking from behind his desk, Darwin said, "With our new understanding about the true origin of the *Alice's Adventures in Wonderland* text, I believe that we can agree that it demands a careful analysis—perhaps a new interpretation. Now that we realize that the text might have arrived from some unknown source using Miss Liddell as a medium while in the throes of a Delphic-like trance—a modern day Pythia—we need to make an effort to understand the true origin and meaning of what at first appears to be clever nonsense. What induced her trance? Who sent the message? Why was it directed to Alice instead of someone else? These and many other questions now confront us. The main question at the moment is what shall we do about it?"

Dodgson now understood where this was going. He realized that once future scholars found out the true source of Alice's story there would be no end of their hypotheses and interpretations of this psychic phenomenon. He wondered if it would be better to confess this to the reading public or just keep pretending this was simply a literary production of his own fancy.

After a few moments Dodgson made his decision and interrupted Darwin. "Excuse me, Mr Darwin, I have another important confession to make. I hope you will all be able to keep my confessions in trust."

"But of course! I'm sure that we are all quite capable of keeping a secret." He looked at the others, who all nodded their ascent. "Please, proceed, Mr Dodgson."

Dodgson spoke to Alice first. "Alice, my dear, in light of the possible seriousness of what we are discussing, I feel that our friends should know the circumstances of the complete story—and not just the first part of it that happened in 1862."

He turned to Darwin and said, "It is important to know that the original transmission to Alice was much shorter than the book that Macmillan published for me in 1865. I expanded it after a second incident in 1863 when Alice once more passed into a trance-like state and received the second, and final message.

"I combined the two to make up the published version, which is almost double the length of the 1862 message. It includes a few additional chapters, including Chapter VII, which I called 'A Mad Tea-Party'. So, the published text is composed of two independent messages received by Alice— other than a few minor corrections that I have continued to make on my own—spelling, grammar, punctuation, and an occasional word replacement—it's complete."

"But every word might be important!" Darwin protested.

"I understand," Dodgson said. "Don't despair. I seldom ever throw anything away. I always keep a record of any later deletions, revisions and additions. I use one of the defective 1865 editions that was returned to me to mark in the text any changes I have since made. I can lend you that copy. I would insist on your returning it, of course."

Darwin sighed in relief. "You had me worried there for a minute, Mr Dodgson. Thank you very much. I shall certainly return it. I'm sure that all of us would like to know about the circumstances of the second transmission. Might you be willing to tell us about it?"

"Of course. This happened in 1863. I maintain a studio in Oxford atop my Christ Church rooms where I have it provisioned with various draperies, furniture, and props that I sometimes use to photograph my subjects. I had hung on a wall a rather faded and chipped backdrop of a painted forest scene that I had acquired from the creditors of the old City of London Theatre, once located in Norton Folgate, after the theatre had closed. At that same time I also acquired a papier-mâché mask, in similarly tattered, but serviceable condition, for Bottom when his head had been transformed into that of an ass. All I needed was an appropriate Fairy Queen and someone to wear the mask. I naturally thought of Alice in the role of Titania and I twisted Duckworth's arm to don the asinine mask. I dressed Alice up as the fairy queen.

"Miss Prickett delivered Alice at the appointed time in mid-afternoon for the sitting. Earlier in the day the weather had been fine, with lovely sunlight shining through the large studio windows, perfect for taking photographs. However, by the time I had everyone costumed and in place a storm had gathered over Oxford and the sunlight was too poor to take pictures, so we waited for about twenty minutes, hoping that the sun would reappear. Suddenly, there was a deafening clap of thunder and a flash of brilliant lightning, the shock of which was Alice's falling into the same trance-like state that she had experienced in 1862. I recognized this by her tone of voice and strange cadence and grabbed a pencil and blank notebook I had in the studio to record dates, names, and exposure numbers, and recorded as best I could everything she said over the next three hours.

"It was again the same story of her Underground adventures continued, strangely twisted and enhanced, with new characters and new wondrous images and word-play! It was as if my *Alice's Adventures under Ground*, the text that I first gave Alice as a token of that unforgettable afternoon, was reflected into another world, and a sequel or missing information was supplied back to Alice, with a remarkable persistence! Such instances are unheard of in the medium world, I am sure.

"I combined the two messages into what became the published version of *Alice's Adventures in Wonderland*, with the obvious exception of the prefatory poem and the last few pages where Alice's sister imagines Alice's dream, which belong to me."

After this account Darwin spoke. "So, based on what you have told us, we can reasonably assume that the entire published account is a very close approximation of the message that Alice received, in two parts, separated by a year."

"Yes."

Darwin continued, "Since there were two other adults in the studio in 1863 there are viable witnesses to these strange events."

"Yes," Dodgson nodded. "And the first event in 1862 was witnessed by my friend Duckworth, and by Alice's two sisters. The sisters were too young to be able to verify much and would be discounted. The second time it happened, both Duckworth and Miss Prickett were present. Once Alice had awakened from her trance we told her what happened—and found that she did not remember most of the vision as she did not remember it the first time. We decided it was best to keep both cases as a secret between the four of us, so that there would be no possibility of damaging Alice's reputation. We didn't want any suggestion of madness to follow her."

"Did you ever get to take the photograph you had wanted?" Darwin asked.

"No. Proper sunlight never returned."

"What happened to the backdrop and props, including Bottom's mask?"

"I destroyed them several years ago. They were already in bad repair and were just taking up scant room in the studio."

"Based on these revelations," Darwin said, "I believe that we should approach the entire text as a natural—or perhaps even a supernatural—phenomenon. We can analyse it as a composite message emanating from the same source using all standard methods of scholarly analysis—as we would do with any ancient manuscript or Babylonian cuneiform tablet.

"Even before the knowledge about the text was revealed here today, I had suggested to Mr Wells and Mr Dalton that we should take a good look at the text to see if there are any clues in it—clues that would elucidate its real message, which, frankly, eludes all of us. Mr Dalton, please inform us of your current observations."

"I did a little word study here," said Dalton, taking out his notes as they rejoined the discussion. "I wish I had a machine that searches for words! My results are somewhat interesting, if baffling. I searched for the word 'wonder' and its variants. This is what I found:

- When she thought it over afterwards, it occurred to her that she ought to have *wondered* at this, but at the time it all seemed quite natural.
- "I *wonder* how many miles I've fallen by this time?"
- "But do cats eat bats, I *wonder*?"
- ...*wondering* how she was ever to get out again.
- "I *wonder* what I should be like then?"

- "Oh, my poor little feet, I *wonder* who will put on your shoes and stockings for you now, dears?"
- "I *wonder* if I've been changed in the night?"
- "It *is* a long tail, certainly," said Alice, looking down with *wonder* at the Mouse's tail.
- "—Dinah! I *wonder* if I shall ever see you anymore!"
- "Where *can* I have dropped them, I *wonder*?"
- ...no *wonder* she felt unhappy.
- "I do *wonder* what *can* have happened to me!"
- "I *wonder* what they'll do next!"
- "—how *is* that to be done, I *wonder*?"
- ...and *wondering* what to do next.
- "How I *wonder* what you're at!"
- Alice joined the procession, *wondering* very much what would happen next.
- "They're dreadfully fond of beheading people here: the great *wonder* is, that there's any one left alive!"
- "...you're *wondering* why I don't put my arm round your waist."
- "Does the boots and shoes!" she repeated in a *wondering* tone.
- Alice said nothing; she had sat down with her face in her hands, *wondering* if anything would *ever* happen in a natural way again.

"So, as you can see, I found twenty instances of 'wonder' inside the Wonderland book. All of them are verb-based, denoting loss or puzzlement, most of the time in sadness—and never in happiness. Of those, eleven are given in the first person as 'I wonder'.

"The word 'Wonderland' is never mentioned in the book as a self-name of the underground world by any of its inhabitants. Moreover, there isn't even a single instance of 'wonderful' or 'wondrous'—and nothing indeed that can be addressed in this way! 'Wonder', of course, is a Germanic word by origin; a child prodigy there is called a 'Wunderkind'. I could not find any synonymous Latinate 'miracle' or 'marvel', or any derived words of those roots either. The reason is obvious: nothing in the *Alice* text qualifies as miraculous or marvellous. 'Wonderland' is *not a land of wonders*—it is just a place where one wonders a lot!

"However, there is a little section in a different tone at the end that has been added by Mr Dodgson, which insists that Alice, in fact, had a dream—and even has her recite this dream to her sister. This is a rather clumsy literary device—such a recitation would take many hours on the same grassy bank, or wherever the girls were sitting on that 'golden afternoon'. Importantly, both instances of 'Wonderland' occur only in this post-scriptum, and were added by Mr Dodgson. This word (as well as the word 'wonderful', also twice repeated here) does not appear anywhere in the text dictated by Alice when in her trance."

"I will read a bit of it: '—what a wonderful dream it had been. Little Alice and all her wonderful Adventures, half believed herself in Wonderland... how she would gather about her other little children, and make their eyes bright and eager with many a strange tale, perhaps even with the dream of Wonderland of long ago.' That's all I found."

"I *wonder*," said Wells, then and smiled to himself. "Yes, and I keep wondering: is 'Wonderland' even a 'land'? Any traditional or modern fairy-tale begins with a map. Children love maps, especially of imaginary places. Many of us drew such maps in our childhood—I know I did. But this text is very obscure on distances and topography: one cannot draw even a schematic map of Wonderland! Distances aren't defined. There is a rabbit-hole; a wood; three houses (the White Rabbit's, the Duchess's, and the March Hare's); the Queen's grounds (with a garden, a croquet field, and a courthouse); and a seacoast where the Mock Turtle lives. The place seems to be spliced together from a few dreamlike images, without any logic. A fairy-tale is logical. In contrast, it always directs a hero into a precise sequence of travels, with rewards and dangers thoroughly prescribed and tied to certain locations. I don't see any resemblance, as suggested by Mr Dodgson, to folkloric tales sung by the ancient bards or poets.

"Most of the humanesque characters in this text are trivial playing-cards: Queen, King, Knave, and so on. At the same time, there is an odd Duchess—who does not belong in the card deck, much like a toy soldier in a box of chess pieces. Outside of Alice's metamorphoses, very few transformations happen—the baby into a pig is the most remarkable and comic one. No serious magic is seen—whether white or black; good or evil. There is no treasure to be found, no quest to be completed, no true villains to be defeated in the end of a story. No elves or fairies are present—and what is the use of a fairy-tale book without elves or fairies? It is a rather pathetic spirit world!"

Dodgson, rather thin skinned and easily offended, didn't immediately know how to respond to Wells' comments. Were he really the author, he agreed, he would indeed populate Alice's world with fairies, or perhaps grotesque German professors, or even a benevolent genie conveying silly, but poetic instructions. As it was, Alice's text appeared to him as an overwhelming, nightmarish nonsense. The text indeed was saturated with illogical word distortions, as if the English language itself was cut apart, twisted, and reassembled in Alice's brain. If this was a message from the spirit world, then this was certainly not a message from a friendly spirit, he decided.

"As a field zoologist," Darwin interjected, "I was intrigued by the fact that when I took a close view at that strange, unnamed, uncharted world, I could not find any truly magical or even exotic creatures, other than an imaginary Gryphon, based on a classical model (who has no magic) and a Mock Turtle. All of the rest are unremarkable English faunal varieties—a rabbit, a mouse, a frog, hedgehogs, a dormouse—even the flamingoes are ordinary residents of the London Zoological Gardens that most children would recognize. Admittedly, there is a dodo, an extinct bird that lived on the island of Mauritius—but Alice surely had seen its famous painting, which is on display in the Oxford Museum of Natural History."

"That's correct," Alice admitted.

"If this story was just a dream," Darwin suggested, "there would be nothing strange in it: dreams work by incorporating and reshuffling reality. Possibly the same mechanism could be offered for hallucinations induced by chemicals. However, if we allow for a moment that Alice was a medium of some sort, then the message—from whatever source—is definitely heavily garbled as it comes into and through the filters of her brain—her nervous and mental constitution, or even what one might call her soul. It is possible that many, if not most, of her images, are not what were really transmitted to her. I suspect that what she received was likely distorted by her young, sensitive brain and transformed into familiar nursery imagery. Hence Alice's sisters' names appearing in a disguise, which seem to be recruited into this dream-like recombination. This effect is common to hallucinations.

"For instance, in South America, under action of certain herbs or, of course, mushrooms, the Indians encounter and converse with their gods and the spirits of their deceased family members. This is common in many 'primitive' cultures, well-outlined by images familiar to their primitive art and folklore. The Aztecs used *Datura inoxia* for prophesying. The Mazatec Indians in Mexico use *Salvia divinorum*, also known as Seer's Sage; it produces pareidolic hallucinations—inanimate objects such as furniture become animated and talk to one another and walking around!

"A sensation of flight—which the alleged witches commonly confessed they experienced—was induced by belladonna, henbane, or mandrake. We now know that ergot, a fungal parasite of rye crops, causes very deep visions, called St Anthony's Fire—it might have been even used by the Greek revelers in their Eleusinian Mysteries. You hadn't eaten any rye bread that day, had you, Alice?" Darwin smiled at Alice who was listening very intensely, truly engaged, and was somewhat proud to be a focus of this astonishing if disturbing discussion.

"Not that I recall," said Alice. "But that was many years ago and I don't recall what we had to eat on the picnic that day."

"If it is a hallucination or a case of hypnotism, I would like to know how it can imprint a lengthy, well-formed, grammatical text—recall that the Pythia's utterances were brief," said Wells. He was leafing through his copy of Dodgson's book looking for any pages he marked. "Here is something else I wanted to bring to your attention. I went through this book several times again when I noticed an extremely poor *sensory scheme* in the text. Nothing in Wonderland, if we elect to believe that this is the real name of the place, has a *smell*—whether pleasant or not, as if Alice's nose was stuffed. The only time when Alice *tastes* anything is the 'Drink Me' bottle. Its content's taste is so remarkably complex and incongruous ('mixed flavour of cherry-tart, custard, pine-apple, roast turkey, toffee, and hot buttered toast') that it seems to wipe off all tastes after that episode. The basic tastes appear indirectly when Alice thinks: 'Maybe it's always pepper that makes people hot-tempered, vinegar that makes them sour, and chamomile that makes them bitter—and—and barley-sugar and such things that make children sweet-tempered.' The only salty substance is Alice's tears.

"We don't know what kind of soup is being prepared by the Duchess's cook, or that the ubiquitous pepper in that pepper-infused kitchen ever gets into the soup. We don't know the taste of that 'beautiful soup' that the Mock Turtle sings about with such longing. Nothing is known about the taste of Alice's comfits, the Queen's tarts that the Knave is accused of stealing, an 'eat me' cake, or a magic mushroom. I wondered if this strange lack of olfactory senses is compensated by visual ones. But there are very few colours! The Queen's roses are *red*—well, *white* ones that are painted red. The Rabbit is also *white*, as well as his kid gloves. *Blue is* mentioned just once, for the Caterpillar. At least the leaves in the forest are *green* and so is the Mock Turtle's *soup*. There is no *yellow* or *black*. The only *orange* is marmalade (which isn't there anyway—no taste; no colour); and the only time we see *purple* is when the Queen's face turns purple with rage. That's it! A remarkable lack of colour."

"That's an interesting observation!" exclaimed Dalton. "I hadn't recognized this. It might mean that the *Alician* text was distorted in the process of either transmission or reception, since it does not contain the normal visual spectrum of the natural world. I can tell you quite a bit about distorted colours, something that I am very interested in. By some weird trick of fate—or more likely, I suspect, heredity. I was born with a highly abnormal, impoverished colour perception. I say heredity, not just anatomy, since my brother is equally afflicted."

Wells nodded. "As you are well aware, we call your specific affliction 'Daltonism', since you were the first to describe it."

"That's how one achieves immortality, I am sure," smiled Dalton. "Since my early years I was keenly interested in this phenomenon, and it led me to many wonderful experiments in nature about vision, light, and other related issues. Many scholars already in my time—and Wells confirmed it with numerous examples from the 1890s—suspect a reasonable connection between body chemistry and biology. I think that in the future we'll find out how the body's chemistry is controlled. Of course there are only a few types of basic building blocks—atoms and their combinations, the simple or larger molecules. From those, however, all the wondrous diversity of living cells and organisms spring forth."

"I wish it was as simple as that!" interjected Darwin. "Heredity could work through primordial particles collected from body cells to germ-line. But no chemist in my time knows what those are made of. A protein of some kind, perhaps—but we are very far from resolving the issue."

"So are we," said Wells. "Heredity *is* the central point! If medical scholars could improve it, science would have a control over human nature. Imagine how remarkable that would be!"

Alice thought about Mrs Shelley's chilling fantasy, *Frankenstein, or the Modern Prometheus*, and shuddered. She was intrigued by Dalton's strange affliction, and asked the old scientist: "Could you please explain to me why you don't see colours, and why this is important? Is your world black and white?"

"I confuse scarlet with green and pink with blue," replied Dalton, "and I do have dulled perception of other colours, like someone with a stuffed nose would have about smell or taste."

"Wasn't there an anecdote about your scarlet Oxford robes?" asked Dodgson. "I don't mean to pry, but I remember reading that you were to be presented to King William IV."

"Oh, that!" laughed Dalton. "Yes; I resisted since as a Quaker I could not wear court dress with a sword! My friend

Charles Babbage assured me that my Oxford Ph.D. robes were sufficient. The trouble was that the Oxford robes are scarlet and as a Quaker I could not wear this colour! So I calmly announced that I could *see* no scarlet. I was presented to the king in scarlet—which I could not tell from green. I think there is something in the vitreous humour of my eyes—like a tint, which selectively absorbs light in the red-green range. A filtering chemical perhaps. I wrote a paper on that subject—and in my will, I stipulated for my eyes to be removed and dissected to confirm this hypothesis."[6]

The image was very vivid. Alice recalled those lines of Queen Gertrude which she memorized in school:

> *"...O Hamlet, speak no more!*
> *Thou turn'st mine eyes into my very soul*
> *And there I see such black and grained spots*
> *As will not leave their tinct."*

"Well, I am long dead in your time," Dalton continued nonchalantly. "1866 is exactly one hundred years from my birth. That does not disturb me at all—hopefully, I have lived to a ripe old age. But I worry whether they had followed my instructions: I told Mr Darwin that I would be delighted to read the dissection report."

"We couldn't locate one yet," Darwin smiled. "Your eyeballs could still be sitting in an anatomical cabinet waiting for dissection, dried and dusty. It's true that many such medical conditions are inherited. We need to pay more attention to those oddities, as they could serve to mark the trajectory of heredity through generations. But let us now get to the point; we were talking about Alice's remarkable imagery."

"That *is* the point," insisted Dalton. "Alice's sensitivity to certain influences must be a material feature of her human body! Unlike many of your contemporaries, I do not hold with the supernatural fashion and I do not believe in ghosts or the spirit world. This world is built of atoms—and their emanations such as light and magnetism, that's all. We need to study carefully all the imagery in Alice's account, as we have just started to do. We should run it against all the hallucinatory events known to medicine—and tie it to nervous reception chemistry. I am hopeful that Mr Wells will be able to provide us with the medical knowledge of his more advanced era that is needed to clarify those mechanisms. We will then have a clue as to what this strange, lengthy hallucination of Alice could have been, and whether it was induced by a chemical or some sort of magnetism."

"I'm not sure we know much about that," Wells said. "I will, of course, upon my return, consult medical authorities on the subject. I think that the reason I looked for colour distortions in the first place, was probably that I developed a sort of colour nostalgia in the recent weeks. In my time-sailing with the Macchinetta, which sometimes takes long hours, there are no colours at all. It appears that the River Times, as I refer to it, does not allow sunlight to penetrate into its flow. It is all shades of black and white; mostly grey—"

Suddenly, Wells stood up and carefully looked at his tiny time-ship standing on the carpet. "Wait a moment!" he cried. "Why, what a fool I am—we all are! I see it clearly now! This colourless, tasteless, meaningless text is a message from the future!"

CHAPTER IV

The Ominous Message

*I*t was hard for Alice to follow the frantic discussion that erupted after Mr Wells' extraordinary pronouncement. "Is it truly possible," she wondered, "that the nonsensical fairy-tale that I dictated while in a trance is actually an encoded message from some future civilization? Which one could it be? Our own dear England, centuries distant? It must at least be some English-speaking country or else Mr Dodgson wouldn't have understood it enough to record it! Australia, perhaps? Or even America?"

As she listened to the scholars' fierce arguments, she felt better. Gone was a recurrent, depressing feeling that she was a victim of some dreadful hallucination, akin to the effect of henbane or Seer's Sage, as Darwin had argued. That would mean her bodily faculties had succumbed to some chemical substance.

"I'm certain that I'm not mad or mentally ill!" she thought. "Not then and certainly not now!" She continued to try to analyse what might have been the cause. "I certainly wasn't under any medicinal influence, like Mr Coleridge, who had a

43

vision or a dream induced by opium!" The lines from one of his poems came to her memory:

> "Where Alph, the sacred river, ran
> Through caverns measureless to man
> Down to a sunless sea.

"I certainly don't like the possibility of some distant hypnotist putting me under his evil spell!" she thought. "And I'm not about to believe some silly idea of spirit-world communication! I'm afraid that that is exactly what Mr Dodgson believes about our picnic four years ago. Now, a message from the future would be something else entirely! That would be most exciting! Still, I ca'n't help wonder if that could possibly be the case!"

Over the next few hours Alice listened attentively to a lengthy and fascinating exchange of ideas and outright fanciful opinions on such things as dream interpretation, madness, future-telling, prophesying, St John's Revelation, and even Nostradamus. Books and encylopaedias were brought in from Darwin's enormous library, consulted, and compared. She knew a little about many of these esoteric subjects and ancient lore from school and from listening to her father discuss the classics. Eventually many pieces of the puzzle seemed to be falling into place.

In the end, there was a consensus that some form of communication of information from the future was possible, especially in light of the obvious fact that they had a flesh-and-blood Time Traveller among them! If a man could actually travel the River Times, why not a signal from the future?

Eventually, Darwin quieted down the discussions and said, "I think that we can now all agree that Alice's case was not a manifestation of just dreams, but rather an *externally induced influence.* We have no evidence of chemical induction by hallucinogenic mushrooms or such substances as peyote or cannabis. Similarly, there is no evidence of such influence from any person or agency, as in the cases of hypnotism, necromancy, shamanism, or spiritism. Frankly, I do not believe that a young girl, even one as bright as Alice, could possibly have made up this tale. These elaborate communications require the mature mind of at least one highly intelligent adult. Mr Dodgson's opinion on spiritualism is noted, but I do not see any hard and verifiable proof that the supernatural world is anything but fantasy. I realize that we will have a quarrel with my friend Alfred Wallace about that. I have personally concluded that Mr Wells' outlandish hypothesis of a message from the future seems the most plausible; let's say the most believable of all the unbelievables."

Dodgson interrupted. "I suspect that a suggestion of communication from the future will seem rather outlandish—even silly or humorous—to most people we might talk to about such a possibility."

"I agree with Mr Dodgson's concerns," said Dalton. "However, we have the Macchinetta sitting right here in front of us! Its undeniable physical existence—and our joint experience in using the apparatus—tells us that time travel to and from future is possible, even if somewhat constrained. Importantly, it does not contradict the laws of nature, because it exists and operates in the natural world. Just because we do not yet understand the laws of nature that allow it does not mean that the laws are not real. They are just new laws that we do not understand and which we need to investigate and define. Therefore, I for one, see no reason why communication along timelines is impossible—with or without a Macchinetta-type device."

"Yes," nodded Wells. "If a traveller can move into his past, so can a message. Sound, light, and electricity, the forces that we harnessed over the ages, and especially in the recent years, all serve for messaging. I am certain that other forces will be discovered."

Dodgson had to agree: "Yes, a soundwave signal goes far; and the savages use quite elaborate drum codes. We know how the Guanches in the Canary Islands communicate by their remarkable whistling language. Mr Wells mentions that sound will be soon transmitted by electric wires akin to the telegraph, coming in a decade from now—a 'telephone' system!"

"What a quaint name," Alice thought. "Even in the future they continue using Greek roots! Maybe not the Germans though—they would surely say *der Fernsprecher*. Why don't they call Mr Dodgson's 'photography' then *die Licht-schreibung*?"

"A beam of light goes as far as we can see it," dreamily continued Dodgson. "Light comes from faraway stars, with incredible speed, and we humans can use it for signaling. The ancients communicated by lighting beacons on mountain-tops."

Alice interrupted the discussion, quoting from Aeschylus:

> *"A gleam—a gleam—from Ida's height,*
> *By the Fire-God sent, it came,*
> *From watch to watch it leapt, that light*
> *As a rider rode the Flame!*[7]

"My father told me that this was how the fall of Troy after the ten-year siege was relayed to Queen Clytemnestra in Argos—in one night, through a string of eight beacons. Ida is the highest mountain on Crete; the Fire-God is Hephaestos, Aphrodite's husband!"

The group applauded lightly at this charming interruption.

Dalton nodded approvingly. "Light and sound are good ways of communcation, but other, more ingenious ways are coming. Your electric telegraph is a marvellous recent invention, its cables now crossing the bottom of the Atlantic Ocean to connect the most prosperous countries of the world! The improved Hughes machine of your time, which I have studied in detail, seems to me a perfect tool symbolic of modern civilization."[8]

Wells interrupted. "An even more remarkable, 'wireless' telegraph is coming soon! I know of amazing experiments by a young engineer named Marconi who, in 1898, will send an electro-magnetic signal though the air. Imagine the possibilities of a future society armed with such a mythical form of communication!"

"Amazing!" Dodgson exclaimed. "While images cannot possibly be transmitted in such a way, a form of Morse code for a wireless 'telephone' would instantly bring one's live voice from Moscow to San Francisco, from Shanghai to Mars!"[9]

"So are we to suspect that Alice's text came to us as such an emanation of wireless nature?" asked Darwin.

"Why not? Surely many forms of natural magnetism could be discovered in the future," said Dalton, "and harnessed for signaling in space—as well as in time."

"Such a signal, to be perceived by a human organism, would be imprinted on the body's receptory organs," said Darwin, "in a way unbeknown to us, but not unlike a regular voice or light communication—through a wave of some ethereal, temporal fluid."

"And, naturally, when such a message comes to a child," noted Wells, "it will manifest itself in a jumble of familiar images—which predominate in Alice's text. This is exactly what we see—and why this text appears to us such a nonsense."

The heated discussion continued, talking about the pervasive, wanton bloodiness and cruelty that Alice's text contained. Sentence before verdict. The threat of decapitation for minor infractions.

At length, Darwin took control of the discussion and asked, "So, is this what awaits us? Is that the shape of a future civilization that sent this message—an Island of Insanity in the middle of the River Times?"

"I noticed something else," said Dodgson, who was again looking carefully through the book just published last year under his pseudonym. "The book contains a lot of statements about children's education. The characters in this tale—not only Alice—constantly attempt to recite well-known poems, and always distort the lines."

"Could that be a signal for our generation?" Darwin asked. "That the school education is destined to fail in the future? That the current system is already beginning to fall apart?"

"Yes, I think so!" said Dodgson. "Please take a look at Chapter IX where the Mock Turtle describes his Underwater school. 'Lessons that lessen' every time! Only now I realize what kind of world I put down on paper that day! On the surface, these word puns appear quite amusing. Indeed, they smartly distort arithmetic as if seen by a bored child. But if one looks deeper, those are the veritable Four Horsemen of Apocalypse!

"Please consider *Ambition*, which is filling the newer generation that strives to survive in a constantly alienated world; a world where faith is crumbling—I'm sorry, Mr Darwin, but a lot of this is due to untimely attacks by your colleagues—where current and even future empires will battle with the aid of even deadlier new weapons. It will be ambition unbridled beyond any of the wildest ambitions of even the Roman emperors or Napoleon himself!

"Next comes *Distraction*—but not by an innocuous game of marbles by a school-child under his desk; nay, the emerging industry of highly immoral still or moving pictures, comic stories, lurid entertainment of the most base kinds; all this made readily available by penny presses; the public omnivorous on cheap writings; the overall decline of morals—the Distraction of all the humankind!

"Now, *Uglification*—yes, and of an utterly barbaric kind! What is so funny in this word? Just look at the modern art, where beauty of Greece and Raphael is all gone. My good friends Ruskin and Rossetti wo'n't be able to hold that dirty flood. Mr Wells' outline of the arts and literature in the 1890s fills me with shame. There is absolutely no guarantee that the advanced (no doubt) twentieth century with its possible flying machines and interstellar engines, will advance in its morals and beauty.

"And the last one—*Derision*—how correct it is! Not only new generations are ambitious, distracted and qualified— they also look with utter Derision at all the great achievements of human spirit, in all spheres that require refinement and nourishment of one's soul rather than instant gratification. Everything delicate and non-feisty goes immediately extinct under a derisive glance of those latter-day barbarians.

"Indeed these four words alone—Ambition, Distraction, Uglification, and Derision—are sufficient to absolutely convince me that Mr Wells is right. No ghost or fairy would mock us as profoundly as the Mock Turtle!"

Dodgson closed his book. He had spoken straight from the heart, his words bubbling up in his mind, in great agitation.

"I agree," said Darwin. "If one intended to imagine the worst degree of mockery—hence the name Mock Turtle—of any educatonal system, one wouldn't be able to produce a more satirical and caustic word-play!"

Wells nodded. "These four words signify four fundamental actions of mathematics—the basis of any educational system, starting from the Egyptians and Pythagoras. Their mockery would clearly embody degradation in its very heart."

"Ambitious and distracted, uglified and derisive pupils—that is not a laughing matter!" cried Dalton. "The Empire will shatter and crumble if those destructive tendencies prevail!"

Darwin sighed: "Yes—it is a nightmare, and I'm afraid that this nightmare is our tomorrow. What do you say, Wells?"

Wells shrugged: "The 1890s are still holding, but surely our century is at a turning point in the development of human civilization. What we see could easily mean that this development will take a disastrous wrong turn."

"Look further!" said Dalton. "What themes are constantly, and rather ominously, showing through the text? Confusion; disorientation; distortion; madness. 'We are all mad here', says the Cheshire-Cat, an embodiment of instability, which appears and disappears as if it is not sure whether it must even remain in this world. Here," he pointed at a book, "'*I wish you wouldn't keep appearing and vanishing so suddenly.*'"

Dodgson agreed, and found another depressing quotation: "'*What the flame of a candle looks like after the candle is blown out?*' This is a very bleak philosophy, so inane and passive that it that sounds decidedly Oriental to me."

"More here, look!" said Wells, "'*It is wrong from beginning to end.*' A very concise statement, indeed!"

Dalton nodded, "It is quite possible that these sentences we keep finding belong to the non-distorted portion of the message, since they are quite lucid and understandable to us. We need to find the way to decipher the entire text!"

"I wish we had a machine that could help to decode this missive," said Darwin. "It would take years for a person to try all possible combinations and permutations of letters and images trying to flesh out the meaningful message from this pile of childish word jumble."

"In fact, a prototype of exactly such a machine could be built right now," Dodgson replied. "Many years ago, MY friend Charles Babbage, a famous polymath, invented an ingenious device he called the Analytical Engine."

"What is that machine?" inquired Wells, quite interested. "Nothing like this yet exists in the 1890s!"

"The device is based on a Jacquard textile loom," replied Dodgson, "and punch cards for input, laced together into a continuous sequence. Ada King, the Countess of Lovelace, and daughter of Lord Byron, helped Babbage in developing his design.[10] Babbage called her 'The Enchantress of Numbers'."

"She surely inherited some talents of her brilliant father," noted Dalton. "What is she doing now?"

"Unfortunately, she died in 1852, at a rather young age," sighed Dodgson. "The Babbage machine was never built."

"I wonder if it would be possible to reach Lady Lovelace with the help of the Macchinetta," said Wells, "and see if she might be willing to work with us—consulting from her years across the time or visiting in person."

"That would be wonderful!" exclaimed Dodgson. "Short of bringing people back from the grave—we can create a society of scholars working together across time! Ada Lovelace was interested in phrenology and mesmerism. She described her approach as 'poetical science'. I am sure she will work with us."

"This Babbage machine could help us to sort and analyse the lucid fragments we find in Alice's text and separate them from nonsense," said Wells. "What we see might indicate that the coded messages of that kind are commonplace among the future people. They possibly even exchange them brain-to-brain, with mind-reading akin to our hypnosis."

"So why don't we see more of those missives?" asked Dodgson.

"It just might be costly to send them, I imagine," said Dalton. "Any message—light, sound, or magnetic—requires energy for transmission. It could be that to travel along the River Times, enormous resources of energy are required. Remember, there is no colour—it is stopped by Time's fabric. Possibly it serves as a filtering fluid for other forms of electric magentism as well."

"If so," said Dodgson, "it might be that Alice's messages are a special attempt directed into our time by the people of—well, we do not know which century! We have no idea how many centuries separate this future civilization from the 1860s."

"Whatever energy it takes," continued Dalton, "future peoples will be able to convey messages by a special kind of magnetism only through technological advances that we cannot even imagine today. Possibly they will have to design giant machines built specifically for that purpose, since the amount of information transmitted would be enormous and on a planetary scale."

It was getting late and Alice needed to leave, so the Time Club decided to adjourn until the next meeting. They felt it should come rather soon.

The River Times

The Time Club met a fortnight later, on the 14th of April 1866. While they were awaiting Darwin and an unknown important guest's arrival, Alice asked Wells and Dalton to tell them more about time travel.

"My experience in time travel with the Macchinetta," Wells began, "is very much akin to river-sailing. The River Times travel, as one might call it, is an amazing pursuit and I have not mastered it yet entirely."

"Please describe it better for me!" begged Alice, unable to control her persistent curiosity any longer. She was told that she wo'n't be allowed to risk time travel herself until she is of age.

"Well, I admit I rarely sailed or even rowed myself," said Wells, "so my metaphors could be mixed. I learned to control the apparatus by an invisible bond that forms when I turn it on. To be precise, the Macchinetta rather controls me; it guides me gently and I somehow intuitively know how to push its levers."

"The Macchinetta apparently manages to read your thoughts, or nearly so," explained Dalton. "It moves like a small sailboat as you point it upstream or downstream. Incidentally, I've begun writing a small book of instructions on time-sailing, which I hope will be useful to others who might have occasion to travel on it. Time, like a river's natural course, seems to make bends around unseen banks or objects. As depths change you can see shoals. Light reflects on its surface as would light on water. Speed varies; sometimes you unexpectedly stop for some hidden reason. Its current abruptly rocks you and turns you around. Apparently, there are limits on where it can take you."

"You can observe changes in the time's high sky," said Wells dreamily. "Perhaps the sky reflects the atmosphere above peace and war. Sometimes you can see what appears to be reeds and rushes along the dimly discernible banks. Most of the time it is a very tranquil and pleasurable experience."

"How fast can you move through time?" inquired Dodgson, fascinated by these poetic but utterly realistic descriptions. He never attempted it himself again after he had been taken by Wells to the time of his childhood.

"It takes about two minutes to pass through a year; sometimes a bit longer," said Wells. "Today, as I travelled from 1898 to 1866, I enjoyed a good hour of peaceful and pleasant sailing. The time weather, if you can accurately call it that, was quite good. However, on some trips you pass rain; I've even heard thunder!"

"Do you get wet?" interjected Alice.

"No, it only feels like the sensation of rain striking you," responded Wells. "You don't need to wear a raincoat or take an umbrella. It's quite pleasant; like a vivid dream of rain."

"As one sails along," explained Dalton, "one can feel changes in light, temperature, and wind velocity; some time segments are darker, cloudier, and emptier, while others bristle with energy and are extremely bright and wonderfully fresh. One can sense colder undercurrents that change your mood; sometimes you feel invigorated passing some stretches and others fill you with desperation and dread. It is not always a pleasant travel, but it is invariably an incredibly interesting one. The same pattern is never repeated!"

"Are there rocks or reefs?" asked Alice.

"Nothing dangerous for the Macchinetta, I think," said Wells seriously, "but the River Times has some deeper and rapid places. Its banks, as far as we perceive them, are akin to rocks and sand and reeds; at many points it is hard to moor."

"Time as one perceives it on the River Times is absolutely silent and colourless, unless you want to take the scientific fact that white contains all colours," noted Dalton. "It's quite like inhabiting a black and white photographic negative."

"Do you eat and drink in your trip?" asked Alice, who was always interested in eating and drinking.

"Well, the machine provides no food." Wells chuckled. "I take some biscuits, cheese and water with me when I plan to travel for hours. Once I arrive I venture into local pubs. They are always available anywhere—*anywhen*—I go in good old England, though the quality of fare can sometimes be a disappointment."

"You are fortunate that you are constrained within civilized years," smiled Alice. "It could be quite different if you went back to William the Conqueror's era or to the Druids or cave people!" Alice thought for a moment, then added, "Do you need to wear a period costume?"

"So far, that hasn't been a problem, but you are correct; it might well be necessary if one was to travel back into distant time!" Wells responded. "It might be dangerous if the populace decided you were a witch or something of the sort!"

"Do you think your travel can disturb time?" asked Dodgson.

"That's a good question and a troublesome concern. From my limited time-sailing experience with Mr Wells," said Dalton, "I conclude that the Time probably exists in myriads of parallel flows, each akin to a road lane or a railroad track. As I join Wells on travelling to my past, the fabric of our timelines coalesces. As we move to my future, we have to switch the traffic lanes to Wells' timeline and follow the same lane he came by."

"People always disturbed time," shrugged Wells. "To live is just like venturing into a sea which never is the same. Why, *nothing* is ever the same. Nature changes all the time. The human body changes. Predictability and chaos are both competing in nature. Timelines, I believe, are also not fixed. Anyone's movements, at any time, can throw a spanner into its mysterious mechanism."

"And every time we take a ride we see changes," added Dalton. "We never return into exactly the same situation; there are always a few changes. It is natural, just like changes in the weather."

"How do you land?" asked Dodgson.

"I direct the Macchinetta toward a certain time and place, but on the River Times one cannot always safely approach the shore," explained Wells. "Its current sometimes is too fast and banks are too muddy or too steep. The apparatus itself chooses a good time-place location to land. In fact, Darwin's house was found by trial and error to be of the best and safest landings in these years. It remains a good anchorage for decades."

"It seems important to me that you both describe your incredible travels in riverine terms," said Dodgson. "Rivers are always somewhat special and strange. Perhaps it is not by chance that this message came to Alice during a boating trip."

Dalton nodded in agreement. "It might be," he said, "that the human body becomes more sensitive to such messages while meditating on a river as quiet as the Isis."

"Such theories exist about communication with the spirits," informed Dodgson. "I know you are skeptical about that, but they say that a good contact requires a certain combination of external conditions and a medium's own efficient state of trance."

"Maybe what you and others deem to be spirits are other time travellers?" Wells suggested half-jokingly. "I cannot believe we are the only people travelling on the River Times. After all, someone dropped the Macchinetta, so there must be more of those riders."

"But why don't you encounter them if they also travel to the past?" asked Alice.

"Yes, " admitted Dalton, "there seems to be no boat traffic on the River Times. Perhaps we do not see them since they travel on different time lanes, or move with a different speed."

"Or they somehow make themselves invisible to us," smiled Wells. "Surely with some chemicals available to future people, they could make their bodies transparent, like real ghosts."

"I wonder," said Dodgson, thinking about communication-through-time theory, "could the device—the Macchinetta itself—assist in attuning our generation and preparing it for a better possible contact with the future? It may not be an accident that Wells found it in the antiquity shop. He could have been meant to find it in 1898, exactly like Alice was meant to receive the messages in 1862 and 1863. These events might be connected."

"Interesting!" said Wells. "Now that you mention it—remind me, please, on what date was the first Alice's message received?"

"The 4th of July 1862," said Dodgson and Alice at the same time.

"In the mid-day, between eleven and four in the afternoon," Dodgson added.

"Same day!" exclaimed Wells. "It was exactly on the 4th of July 1898, close to noon, when I saw, and immediately purchased the Macchinetta in that West End shop! What a co-incidence!"

"I find it hard to believe in co-incidences anymore," noted Dalton, grimly. "It surely looks as if some agency is at work."

"It might be," said Dodgson, "that mid-summer days have something in their fabric that allows better contact—or transfer—between time lanes. One immediately recalls *Midsummer Night's Dream*. Shakespeare, with his sensitivity of a genius, could have felt that the physical transparency of English mid-summer lends itself to all sorts of mystical influences. I always thought it is possible that there exists an 'eerie' state in which a person is conscious of the presence of fairies—or a form of trance, in which, while he is conscious of actual surroundings, and apparently asleep, his immaterial essence migrates to other scenes, in the natural world, or in Fairyland, and is conscious of the presence of fairies.[11] What many before and after Shakespeare thought to be fairy-world contacts, could have been attempts of contacts from the future as well! Maybe it wasn't by chance that the second message reached Alice in summer 1863 when she was dressed as Titania!"

"It could be," proposed Wells, "that Alice's vision was conveyed by a radiation that emanated from some future device, a message-machine of an incredible force penetrating the flow of the River Times itself! Again, we have no way of knowing how much effort those who sent it put into this message—or in building the Macchinetta."

"Could the Macchinetta be a unique artifact?" asked Dodgson. "Like an art piece by Leonardo? A machine created by a brilliant craftsman of the future?"

"Well," said Dalton, "it would be presumptuous to think that this future civilization kindly gifted to us their only time-transportation device!"

"But perhaps it is the only one they have!" said Alice. "The message I received might be a cry for help! Perhaps their civilization is dying—and this could be a life-boat thrown to us—to save the human race!"

At that very moment, they saw Darwin enter with his guest.

"We are here at last!" Darwin exclaimed to the members of the Club. "I'm sorry that you have had to await our tardy arrival. Please, let me introduce my second cousin, Mr Francis Galton, whom I welcome as our new member. Francis is a man of many talents and he has already taken a few trips with Mr Wells. He is extremely excited by the opportunities of time-sailing."

"I love it!" exclaimed Mr Galton, a younger, more choleric man than his distinguished cousin. "Mr Wells sometimes even allows me to control the Macchinetta's mysterious levers."

"We piloted it together," said Wells, "around the shoals, as I took Mr Galton to visit my own time, about which he had mixed feelings; he expected much more technical and moral progress, and I'm afraid what he saw was not entirely to his high expectations."

"What is also remarkable," exclaimed Galton, "is that the Macchinetta does not run out of fuel! There are no visible tanks or chambers that could house combustible material. I believe it may be powered by some unknown type of magnetism, possibly emanating from Earth's natural field generated by its molten iron core. If correct, then it could provide future generations with an endless source of energy!"

"A very reasonable possibility," nodded Dalton. "Are you an engineer by profession, Mr Galton, or do you teach physics?"

"No, sir, I am just an avid amateur in all matters of natural science, though not a rival to my cousin Charles, the greatest naturalist of our time. Frankly, he finds many of my pursuits outlandish!"

"I certainly do," smiled Darwin, "and all the same, I value your incessant energy and remarkable thinking! You inherited more imagination from our common grandfather, Erasmus, the great polymath, than I did. This is why I gladly confided in you, not only concerning time-travel, but also on our considerations pertaining to Alice's extraordinary, even outlandish, text. Please tell us now, Francis, what you have discovered on your own!"

It was obvious to all that Mr Galton was overexcited. He nervously paced several times around the study almost knocking down an expensive model of *HMS Beagle* that would fall right on Alice's barnacle jars. Fortunately, she caught it just in time to avoid a disaster. Finally, Galton composed himself and said, "Gentlemen—and Alice, of course—I have met many a great scholar in this house, but it is not an ordinary trivial occurrence when one meets a time-traveller from the end of our century—and a recipient of a message from an even more remote future! Naturally, I have read Mr Dodgson's clever book, as practically everyone in England has done! In fact, I own and treasure a first edition in which he has kindly inscribed a clever acrostic poem with my name. He wants me to return it, but I could never part with it, no matter if some of the images are a bit smudged, as he insists."

"Do hold onto it, Francis," said Darwin, smiling. "It might be worth fifty pounds one day." Everyone except Galton laughed at his silly joke.

"That is not a joking matter!" insisted Galton. "The first edition of the First Message from the Future Generations might well become priceless in a hundred years! Excuse my possible blasphemy, Mr Dodgson, but this would be like owning an original scroll of St Paul's epistles!"

"Or, rather, St John's Revelation," grimly noted Dalton.

"Indeed!" said Galton. "Charles kindly allowed me to read his notes and minutes of your previous meeting. Before coming here, I conducted some analysis on my own. As I examined the text, it seemed to me that the thoughts of the future scholars who transmitted this message back to 1860s, became embedded inside Alice's mind, as if uttered by the story's imaginary characters. This is how I explain many nursery-style images and fairy-tale events. Confronted with alien signals, Alice's brain generated familiar views—a garden, the White Rabbit's house, a tea-party table, a croquet-ground—effectively translating the message into a more familiar environment. However, many ominous themes pervade these quaint settings, and I would like to elaborate on some of those, if I might."

"Please, Francis," Darwin said, "by all means go ahead."

"Thank you. Here are my preliminary hypotheses and assumptions, my modest glosses on that revelatory text, which, I am sorry to say, is full of disorientation, insanity, blood, tears, and all kinds of rather ominous, dark nonsense!"

CHAPTER VI

Mr Galton Has a Plan

*M*r Galton dumped an impressive heap of notes on top of Darwin's desk. "First," he began, in a scholarly manner, "consider the theme of insanity—of madness, if you will—it is very prominent in Alice's message from the future. This is bluntly expressed by the dialogue between the Hatter, who has earlier been described by the Cheshire-Cat as being mad, and an equally mad March Hare. The image of a mad Hatter obviously alludes to the familiar idiom 'mad as a hatter'. In addition, please note what the Cheshire-Cat had earlier pointed out: *'We're all mad here. I'm mad. You're mad'* and *'You must be, or you wouldn't have come here'*! Alice declares: *'I don't want to go among mad people!'* The obvious implication is that our future society has descended into madness."

"What might be the reasons for that?" asked Dodgson.

"There are many!" said John Dalton, who had been listening attentively. "Think of air pollution generated by new industries! It already plagues your cities, London first and foremost among them. Why, the saying 'mad as a hatter' itself is a reflection on mental disease common in his profession, it appears likely that it might be due to mercury poisoning."

"Indeed," Galton agreed. "As humanity moves further from Nature, it endangers its collective sanity through the physical action of chemicals it manufactures. These emerging compounds are being discharged into the air we breath, the food we eat and feed to our livestocks, and perhaps most criticaly important into the water. I suspect that this will inevitably bring changes—unnatural, unwanted, and most likely uncontrolled! Quoting this mysterious message again, from Chapter I, *'if you drink much from a bottle marked "poison", it is almost certain to disagree with you, sooner or later.'"*

Darwin nodded and then said, "Note also that the *pepper* motif in the Duchess's house. Chapter VI says, *'There was certainly too much of it in the AIR.'* It could signify an extremely dirty atmosphere of the future Earth, full of irritant chemicals and becoming unbreathable, even affecting fertility and heredity—hence that baby who turns into a pig! The incessant sneezing of everyone save the Cheshire-Cat might well portend severe allergies and other pulmonary diseases specific to humans.

Wells chimed in, quoting, *"'What became of the baby?'—'It turned into a pig.'—'I thought it would.'* There might also be unexplored effects of electricity and magnetism, introduced into industry and everyday life over the next centuries, also taking their toll."

"Moreover, what we read in the 'Pig and Pepper' chapter could be Alice's unconscious interpretation of *chemical warfare!*" Dalton added. "Madness of the future could even lead unscrupulous and evil people to poison the air and water, deliberately releasing toxic gases or fluids."

"Among the civilized nations," Dodgson objected, "one could hardly imagine a military use of poisonous chemicals. A cowardly and savage device like that surely would forever damage the honour of any general or officer in charge of such an operation. And it would be to no use, as the other side would surely retaliate in kind."

"Surely such ghastly weaponry is quite unthinkable in our time!" cried Alice in horror.

No one offered any assurances, but rather sat quietly trying to imagine the unthinkable: a chemical war of the future.

Galton was the first to break the silence. "As the book says, *'It is wrong from beginning to end.'* In addition to *madness*, the theme of bloody executions is quite pervasive, rapidly increasing in intensity toward the end of Alice's message. This motif was transformed, in our brave little medium's mind, into a playing-card Kindgom of Hearts, with its red-coloured cardboard characters—Queen, King, and Knave cards. Alice herself in her vision appears as a hero battling these evils. I am not sure where all these images come from, but they look rather traditional."

"Might this be an influence of those Continental fairy-tales that I liked so much as a child? They have brave girls in them," suggested Alice who has been listening very carefully to this remarkable analysis and was eager to contribute to the discussion.

"Are you thinking about Little Red Riding Hood?" smiled Dodgson.

"Oh, no; that is too childish; why not Hoffmann's *Nuß-knacker und Mausekönig*? It has a girl protagonist, Marie Stahlbaum. She fights an evil Mouse King. Or, ever better, my favourite—Hans-Christian Andersen's *Snow Queen*, with its brave Gerda!"

ALICE AND THE TIME MACHINE

"Very good!" said Dodgson approvingly. "You might add Count Gozzi's *commedia dell'arte* plays which we saw years ago—in particular, his *L'amore delle Tre Melarance*, which takes place in a fairy-tale play-card kingdom."

"Whatever the source of fairy-tale imagery that the mesage evoked in Alice's brain," continued Galton, "card games aren't nearly as aggressive as the Queen of Hearts appears. This evil image carries deep and disturbing information about future society. I see despotic emperors or dictators who will arise again to enslave humankind, to place sentence before verdict, to chop everyone head off—with or without a reason! Furthermore, I think that the *underground* location of Wonderland—we may even call it Underland—is rather important. Alice's perception gives us a rabbit-hole, but this natural tunnel might also be a reference to our new London Underground—one of the most amazing achievements of civilization today. Since its first Metropolitan line opened between Paddington to Farrington, this Underland became a major defining feature of the great city."

"I thought of this!" said Dodgson. "At the same time, the rabbit-hole descent clearly reflects Dante's travel to the *Inferno*—only Alice had no guiding Virgil. Surely they saw quite different figures!"

To everyone's surprise, Alice suddenly quoted a passage:—

> *"Poi ch'innalzai un poco più le ciglia,*
> *vidi 'l maestro di color che sanno*
> *seder tra filosofica famiglia.*
> *Tutti lo miran, tutti onor li fanno:*
> *quivi vid' ïo Socrate e Platone,*
> *che 'nnanzi a li altri più presso li stano.*[12]

"I have read some of the book with my Italian teacher," she added. "The *Inferno* is infernal indeed—it gets furiouser and furiouser as you descend! At least Dante put all the Greek philosophers into his First Circle."

"But what would be the significance of having an underground kingdom in this text?" inquired Darwin.

"Oh, *that* is obvious!" said Wells. "The Future people are likely to live underground. As Ice Ages wane, climate warms, and the planet enters a period of atmospheric disturbance. It might very soon become impossible to live aboveground. In addition, industrial pollution—that pervasive pepper of the Duchess's Kitchen—will make breathing harder and harder. All this, and the emerging warfare—flying bombs and aerial machines—could force humakind permanently down deep mineshafts. Men would become Kobolds and Gnomes of ancient legends. Our Underground trains are just the first step toward Dante's Inferno!"

Alice's mind was rushing through the Greek myths she liked so much: "But there were so many others before Dante who descended into nether worlds! Odysseus went down to Hades to get his instructions from Tyresius; and Orpheus went after Euridice, poor thing—and Persephone comes and goes all the time."

"And Osiris, and many others in chthonic myths, so common to both Greeks and Egyptians," nodded Dalton. "In fact, as I look now at the Egyptian connection, I come to another obvious fact we missed completely."

"What is it?" asked Dodgson.

"It is that, on the 4th of July 1862, you, dear sir, and your party, rowed near Oxford on a portion of Thames called *Isis*!"

"Yes!" cried Wells. "Isis, mother of Horus, the goddess of magic and also a benefactor of children. How fitting! Another clue to the message's addressee."

Again, Alice spoke up, this time playfully quoting from her own underground adventures:—

"It seems to be a letter, written by
The prisoner—to somebody... But who
Is it directed to?—It isn't directed
At all!—Though this be madness,
Yet there is method in't."

"Perhaps it was just directed at Oxford," suggested Dodgson, always an Oxonian. "If I were a denizen of the future, I would aim my shot at the most educated place in the world. There are scholars versed in all kinds of languages, from Assyrologists to Sinologists who can decode all the details."

"Why not Cambridge? It is a more suitable place for natural sciences scholars who would want to explore the physics of the signal transmission and perception," said Darwin, who was a Cantabrigian; his Bachelor of Arts degree was from Trinity College.

"Or maybe the message was indeed directed at Alice personally," suggested Dalton. "Do not underestimate the sensitivity of children! Adult perception and other talents get dulled with age."

"Yes," agreed Dodgson. "After all, it looks like Alice will be the most well-known English child on the planet for generations! That, provided the craze of *Alice's Adventures in Wonderland* does not subside. And Mr Wells told me that it doesn't: he says the book will have 150,000 copies published by 1898![13] I might see some substantial profit from the royalties."

"There is something remarkable in this text," noted Darwin, "if it could hold such allure on a future reader. But please, Francis, continue!"

"Finally," said Galton, thumbing through his notes, "in addition to the highly disturbing themes of *madness, executions*, and the underground world, there is a very peculiar motif of distorted time. We see that in 'The Mad Tea-Party' of Chapter VII. I feel that this subject is extremely important to the text—the message—but I need to work on it further as I am not qualified to comment on actual physics of time, which, I believe, is very little known to science."

"It is still a deep mystery in my age," admitted Wells. "I know there is some new mathematics behind time-space theories. The Macchinetta, I am sure, should help us to explore these uncharted waters!"

"I feel that something disastrous might be approaching," said Galton rather gravely. "All religions and revelations tell about the End of Time. Could St John or Nostradamus receive similar messages from the future? We can easily guess that Time *has* ended—has stopped—at the Mad Tea-Party table. Relationships of the fantastic characters with Time are very strange: '*I dare say you never even spoke to Time! ... He wo'n't stand beating.*'"

"This might indicate that something happened to its fabric in that future where the message came from," remarked Dalton. "Maybe humankind will meddle with the very nature of Time? Such tinkering can be dangerous in the presence of high energies."

"The Tea-Party," said Galton, "definitely finds itself in a time-loop: '*what happens when you come to the beginning again?*' And, the worst thing is that, I fear, the Science itself is being mocked at the same time. Listen to this '*you might do something better with the time than wasting it in asking riddles that have no answers.*'"

"This concludes my observations so far. Thank you, Charles, for this opportunity to address the Time Club, of which, I trust, I am now a proud and full member. I predict that when all our deliberations are made public, the sensation produced will be enormous—more than when Champollion presented his results from the Rosetta Stone. I envision that this small book will be subjected to enormous scrutiny by many scholars for decades!"

"Thank you very much, Francis!" Darwin responded. "And *I* envision, in my turn," said Darwin, as he tried, rather clumsily, to lighten the atmosphere, "that scientific volumes will be published by my fellow zoologists on all the minutiae of Gryphon and Mock Turtle, and especially the Cheshire-Cat, whose immortal speeches will be translated into dozens of languages—from Latin to Russian to Appalachian English!"

No one smiled.

"Don't jest!" said Wells. "I can see how learned journals and academies will compete for the latest interpretations of this first message from the future in human history."

"Well, we cannot wait for those academies," suggested Dodgson. "We should further pursue the efforts in decoding Alice's Message! And it would be interesting to search for other such signals—other texts! But where and when?"

"I think of places such as Dublin or Prague, long known for their tradition of mystical contacts," said Wells.

"I think of Stonehenge," said Darwin.

"I think of Delphi and the Pyramids," said Alice.

"There might be more of such 'thin places' in our world where the accessing of future missives is easier than in the others," said Dodgson. He smiled: "The Spiritualists could possibly help us."

"Gentlemen! This is all well and interesting;" said Galton quite seriously, "but we might not have much time for scholarly pursuit. You forget the urgency and tragic tone of the message. Even if we understand only a few sentences of this text it is still very disturbing. Consider! Alice received her first message in 1862 and then again in 1863, and Wells obtained the Macchinetta in 1898. For 35 years, nothing was done on our side to change the existing situation! They are clearly asking for help—we need to act!"

"But what *can* we do?" asked Darwin. "We cannot change the course of history!"

"Maybe we can!" exclaimed Galton. "I have a plan for us— we need to develop a well-conceived programme for doing exactly that!

"Alice's Message clearly shows us the tragic face of the future—which is, it is not hard to guess, highly techno-logical. If they did not have machines, they wo'n't be able to penetrate time with emanations such as Alice's signal and devices such as the Macchinetta. It is also not hard to guess that they had, or still have, a man-made Apocalypse—a major war-like conflict, maybe permanently waging—a new world-wide Napoleon with hideous weaponry we cannot even imagine; loss of direction; total insanity; a lot of blood. Maybe even time stops—and space collapses, and things change their very shape, in a global bout of metamorphopsia. Their *time is out of joint*—literally, not metaphorically.

"What we need is to engineer an immediate turn in historical events so this future will not come to pass. We do not know how many centuries ahead it lies, but they chose us. It cannot be by chance—which means that our time, the nineteenth century, remains the most reasonable and lucid compared to the centuries to come! Any real change in history comes through science and invention, through Galileos and Faradays. Too often, however, their efforts remained unappreciated and forgotten; too often Dark Ages descended on humankind. Our destiny, gentlemen, is to correct the course of human history! And we are given the tool. We have the Macchinetta!

"I do not believe it was just abandoned in 1898 by some visitor as one drops his watch walking on a heath, or forgets his basket after a roadside picnic. It is clear that Wells was led to it, and they—whoever provided it—want us to use this extraordinary tool. We can assist Wells in travelling along the nineteenth century as far as the Macchinetta will take us. We will draft intellect from time both upstream and downstream—we will find as many of those scholars who died unknown and unrecognized as we can. We will work with them to create a network of minds, theories, and practical achievements.

"We will combine brilliant insights of the 1820s—like yours, Dalton—with remarkable discoveries of the 1890s— which you will deliver, Wells. We will make sure that marvellous ideas are not forgotten and appear on time—not delayed like your 1859 treatise, Charles, which waited for twenty years because some deemed it to be too dangerous!

"More than that, we'll need to overhaul today's chaotic management of that most precious commodity—the human intellect! We will draft our Army of Talent from all over the world to England, today in 1866, and in all other decades we can reach. We will make England the place of enlightenment rather than political bickering or colonial aspirations.

"We need your Guglielmo Marconi, here and now, Wells— and even before now as far as we can reach downstream. He might agree to come and work with us—slowly and confidentially spreading his wireless signaling back into earlier decades, thus enhancing history in repeating loops—like a spider building its web. We need Babbage's Analytical Engines built in every university, in every decade.

"We need a hundred young Marconis and Babbages! We will select—purchase, if needed!—the brightest children of all races from all over the world; and the best professors to teach them. Oxford and Cambridge will expand a hundredfold to accommodate the human talent—a critical mass unheard of in history—a Plato's Academy magnified and reborn.

"We will, within the biological time allotted us, enhance and direct discoveries—to harness the forces of Nature—light, ether, magnetism—and place those Promethean spirits at our service with new and inventive machines. We will work for the betterment of the human race itself, learning and altering debilitating conditions, and advancing medicine in all fields; we will experiment, explore, and expand. We must become wise advisors to kings and presidents.

"Science must not remain a parlour game it is to-day, and it must not develop in leaps and jolts. Above all, development of the weapons of war by all powers must be completely stopped—too much intellectual energy and human material is siphoned today to armament works of all kinds, fuelling future wars.

"Eventually, society might even choose, instead of the degenerate aristocracy of to-day, to establish a *sophocracy*— a rule of sages. They may even breed the cadre as we breed thoroughbreds—why not?—but now we have no time.

"Together, ultimately, we might be able to push that Sisyphean stone to the hilltop; to switch the Train of History to a new track—or, to use a better metaphor, to change the flow of the River Times!"

Everyone was speechless after listening to this incredible burst of energy as Darwin's cousin described something what would seem completely implausible under regular circum-stances. But everything now was quite irregular.

"Aren't we just too few?" Dodgson asked finally. "Can we even change what destiny the Divine Providence already plotted for us—which, alas, seems to be so bleak?"

"Let us assume," said Galton coldly, "as a working hypothesis, that Providence *wants* us to change history. Otherwise we would not be chosen!"

"And if so," asked Darwin, "what are we going to tell the public? Don't people have the right to know? All this activity that you propose, Francis, cannot go unnoticed—not on that scale. And, if our ultimate goals and the existence of Alice's Message and the Macchinetta are announced to the public, the story will only create panic and latter-day riots. Recall how Priestley, the discoverer of oxygen, was attacked by a mob in 1791 in Birmingham!"

"I thought about it," Galton replied. "We would start with confidential, Freemason-style contacts. We need a very select group first. Today in 1866, it would be maybe several dozen, only the trusted people, chosen with all precautions. Secret societies have been doing it for centuries—we can even pretend we are Rosicrucians or some other kind of Illuminati. Throw in some Swedenborg, that's a good guise. Nobody pays attention to those people."

"I would do the same in my time, and Wells in his, but our cross-temporal contacts will be necessarily limited," said Dalton. "Wells is the only one who can control the Macchinetta, so he can shuttle one person at a time. We will need to establish a network of agents in other decades."

"It may be possible. My first contact with Lady Lovelace was very successful," reported Wells. "She agreed to work with us, and so did Charles Babbage—both in the 1840s and now."

"Another word of caution," said Darwin. "You come from a wealthy family, Francis, but do you intend to finance all this effort by yourself?"

"To equip even a single Physics laboratory costs a small fortune, and we need facilities," said Dalton. "We will have to search for rich sponsors."

"I wish the Queen could help us!" said Alice suddenly, with passion. "Isn't she the most powerful and the richest person in the world? And she surely will understand!"

Everyone looked at her.

"This is reasonable," said Darwin. "If we can get Victoria on our side, it would be a great leverage! But how do we reach the Queen in a clandestine way, not to attract unwanted attention?"

"In fact, this could be done," said Dodgson. "I know that the Queen was interested in the *Alice* book. I think she has read it—and there was confusion; someone sent her instead my next one, *An Elementary Treatise on Determinants*! I think it is a good book, as far as mathematical books go. Also, I know a few people high up in society, since I was taking photographs of their children for a long time. I have no easy access to the Royal Family, but some of my acquaintances are positioned high enough."

"Then let us try to get an audience!" said Galton. "And meanwhile, we had better put all our notes and plans in writing! If the Queen will agree to see us, she would need to read our report first."

CHAPTER VII

Alice Meets the Queen

lice had hoped that her Majesty, Queen Victoria would be enthroned, wearing royal robes when they arrived, with a great throng of courtiers assembled before her, but Alice realized that this was highly unlikely. Together with Dodgson and Wells, they had not even entered through the Buckingham Palace main gate, but rather had been escorted into an inconspicous side passway, up some unremarkable stairs, through some dim, narrow corridors, before finally being ushered into a small, but elegantly appointed, private sitting-room. This was where the most important meeting in Queen Victoria's long reign would take place.

A distinguished elderly man entered and introduced himself. Dodgson recognized the well-known face of Lord Derby, the new Conservative Prime Minister, and one of Christ Church's most illustrious alumni. For Wells, who had travelled back from the future, the Prime Minister was ancient and important history. Lord Derby was in his third ministry, just recently formed in June 1866.

Alice recalled the first lines from the *Iliad* recently translated by Lord Derby:—

> *"Of Peleus' son, Achilles, sing, O Muse,*
> *The vengeance, deep and deadly; whence to Greece*
> *Unnumbered ills arose…"*

Two palace servants brought tea and departed quietly. Some small talk followed, but the Prime Minister did not sound too friendly or happy to be wasting his time on the meeting.

In about twenty minutes, the Queen entered, robed in black, still in mourning. She graciously greeted her visitors. The three men bowed, and Alice curtseyed. Her head was spinning slightly, since it was the first time she had ever seen the beloved monarch close by. The Queen resembled her portraits, but her expression was sad and resolved. "Gentlemen—and young Miss Liddell!" said the Queen. "We have read your report, and we see the situation as of the utmost importance." She stepped over to Alice and took her hand in hers. "My child," she said,"you should have had a ghastly experience as you received and transmitted this revelatory message. We commend your strength and determination. Nine girls out of ten probably would not have survive the ordeal without a serious mental disturbance.

"We had read *Alice's Adventures in Wonderland* last year, but after reading the report we re-read it more seriously this time. First, it appeared rather amusing, in a childish, nonsensical way. However, if what you tell us has even a scruple of truth—then we are bothered immensely by the tone of this text, or rather a powerful vision.

"The technological veracity of a message from the future does not seem to us to be too far-fetched. We have magnetism and telegraph; man's technical abilities are boundless. Less so, it seems, are his abilities to tame savage instincts that have shaken the world so much of late.

"This text—Alice's Message, as you address it in your extensive commentary—appears to be especially, we might say hypnotically, strong and lucid in passages where it depicts wanton blood-letting, as if Dark Ages will dawn on us again. We are not trained in decoding messages; but we doubt that scholarship exists today that would allow one to decode this text in its entirety—if it is what you, gentlemen, deem it to be. Scholars will pore over this little book for many decades, and each era will read into it its own conceptions— as into a Chinese book of divination. We have made our own observations of this text—which everyone still considers belonging to your skilled pen, Mr Dodgson. A nightmare emerges, to signal the upcoming and unwelcome reality.

"Here are a few quotations we have written down," said the Queen as she took out a small note-book with an ivory-plate cover and a silver pencil. "One does not have to be a historian to interpret these words as a blood-chilling evidence of the despotic kingdoms existing in the future—new Cromwells unleashed, or new Bonapartes! Listen!

- "…they don't seem to have any rules in particular…"
- "If I don't take this child away with me… they're sure to kill it in a day or two. Wouldn't it be murder to leave it behind?"
- "Talking of axes… chop off her head!"
- "Off with their heads! … Are their heads off?"
- "…if something wasn't done about it in less than no time, she'd have everybody executed, all round…"
- "…anything that had a head could be beheaded…"
- "They're dreadfully fond of beheading people here: the great wonder is, that there's any one left alive!"

"The great *wonder* indeed!" said the Queen sadly. "So much for a *Wonder*land, Mr Dodgson! Chopping off heads, sentence before verdict? We have been through this in mankind's history so many times over and over. White rose-bush painted red—why, these are Yorks and Lancasters all again. It pains us that we might be destined to repeat the vicious cycle! That is not *our* Pax Britannica!"

A chill went through Alice's body. The memory of the July 1862 vision came back now, and lingered a bit longer than usual. The mad Queen of Hearts—so unlike motherly Queen Victoria—came back to her a pure embodiment of a blind and aimless Fury—one of those evil Greek spirits.[14]

"Mr Tenniel's pictures were much nicer," Alice thought. "Was that image what future centuries are trying to tell us?" she wondered. "The evil incarnate usurping thrones, Caligulas and Attilas reigning free? Will the French terror repeat itself?"

"Your Majesty!" said Wells bravely. "The times are changing. I admit being a staunch Republican myself. I honestly never approved of the archaic, antiquated system of government of our 'crowned republic'. I think that every Englishman—and Englishwoman, too—should be allowed to vote their opinion on the policies."

"Women?" muttered Lord Derby. "Are you telling me that in your future time *ladies* are allowed to vote? My Chancellor of the Exchequer, Mr Disraeli, is just now attempting to pass a Reform Bill, to enfranchise voting by most *men* in urban areas."

"Not in England yet," admitted Wells, "but in a few of the self-governing colonies, yes. New Zealand granted voting rights to women in 1893, and South Australia in 1894. And the Empire did not fall! Your Majesty's reign by end of the century is indestructible. Wars have subsided. The Continent seems to be peaceful enough, notwithstanding German patriotic misconceptions. One hopes that the Englishman will not turn readily enough toward the vague exaltations of modern imperialism.[15] Russia's military is strong but the end is seen even to the Tsar's incessant Great Game—the Afghan boundaries are drawn in the 1880s. Indian mutinies are no more. Your reign is so firm that it is something unprecedented in history. One day I will complete what I always wanted to write, a universal *Outline of History* for the masses—the Victorian Era will be the crowning achievement of all epochs rivaling the Roman Empire only."

"We know only too well how *that* Empire ended," noted Victoria. "Nothing lasts forever—but you have convinced us, Mr Wells. Even if your designs seem outlandish, it appears that Providence—whose hand we see here, no doubt—confided in us the very tool of changing our own Destiny."

"But what tangible proof do you have that your time travel actions could change—or, better, improve—historical events?" asked Lord Derby, grimly.

"I do have proof," said Wells solemnly. "So far I only divulged it to my Club fellows, and I agree it would seem a fantasy, but I swear it is true.

"As soon as the Macchinetta fell to my hands, and I started experimenting with time travel—I decided to see with my own eyes the decisive battles of the Crimean War. It might seem childish for you, but for an English boy who grew up—will grow up!—in the 1870s, the embattled Russian peninsula was—will be—an ancient battlefield akin to a Salamis or a Gaugamela.

"I will not bother you with details, which I can submit as a separate report. I will briefly account for the events. I travelled as a tourist to Russia and reached Sevastopol in August 1898. It is not uncommon in my time to see English tourists in Crimea, paying tribute to the graves of our soldiers. There are over a hundred of those in Sevastopol and

Balaklava. Aimed by a detailed map, I was able to locate the most important positions.

"I pointed my little machine to spring 1855—I wanted to see personally the famous second bombardment on the 9th of April when the Russians lost 6,000 people in one night. It was then a still unknown to me feature of my little marvel that it experiences landing issues—possibly when space-time is disturbed by artillery?—and travels sideways in space. Well, I almost became one of the casualties of the famous night as I landed on the enemy's side—at the Russian Fourth Bastion at the time of the most severe artillery shelling.

"A young Russian artillery officer saw me in my decidedly civilian Jaeger woollen suit as I hanged in the air above the breastwork (the machine lands you gently choosing the substratum). The officer was startled by an apparition and tried to subdue me; in an embrace, we both rolled down to the bottom of the bastion—and this saved us both from the explosion of a good old British cannonball. As soon as I detached myself from the officer, yelling quite unconvincingly 'I am not a spy!' and could reach the crystal levers, I pushed myself away from 1855.

"As I returned safely to my London of 1898, it appeared to me that there was something familiar in the face of the officer who saved me—or, rather, we saved each other since if we did not take that painful tumble he would clearly be killed by that cannonball and become one of those 6,000 victims. I had a feeling I *knew* that face! I could not place it but since I do not know so many Russians I suspected it could be someone famous. He was nearly thirty during the battle of 1855, so he would be in an old man in 1898—and possibly bearded, as beards will come in vogue again in my time. It was too late to visit a library, which I decided to do next morning; but I started looking through my bookshelves for a possible portrait of an elderly, famous Russian—and within ten minutes I found this bearded face!

"You would hardly know him—but you can check and watch! His name is Count Leo Tolstoy. *The Sevastopol Sketches* where he describes the battle—although not our brief altercation—were published in 1855. He is forty years old today, in 1866. His greatest literary pieces are still to be written. His *War and Peace*—about Napoleon's war with Russia—will be published three years from now.

"It is highly possible that there was no such writer in my 1898 timeline *before* I travelled to the Crimea. My memory vaguely tells me that I used to live in a world without Tolstoy. It is incredible to think that if I didn't attempt this reckless visit—if two of us did *not* tumble down these stairs—this second lieutenant would be smashed by the British shelling right here on the 4th Bastion, and our century would lose its most remarkable pen—or some would say, a prophet. I haven't yet attempted to visit him and remind of our improbable encounter."

The Prime Minister remained unconvinced. "The man is mad, your Majesty," he said. "He should be locked up, and that is all I can say. I am sorry, Mr Dodgson and Miss Liddell, but your friend has no proof that he really came from our future. The coins and clothes and this apparatus he shows can be all fake. A clever attempt to influence your Majesty's politics perhaps!"

"Sir—I can bring the most direct proof, even without a risk of offering you to travel with me in person!" offered Wells, exasperated. Turning to the Queen, he said, "Your Majesty could kindly provide me with a note addressed to yourself. I will ask for an audience in 1898. You will surely recognize your own handwriting—and perhaps choose to send a reply."

The Queen smiled and replied, "This would not be necessary. Do not bother the old Queen."

She turned to the Prime Minister. "Lord Derby," she said. "Please give Mr Wells the benefit of a doubt. We tend to believe that his little machine indeed takes him back and forth along our century—as a boat takes one along the Thames."

"It does!" exclaimed Wells. "And with its help, if your Majesty wishes, your reign will play a great role in changing history by enhancing human knowledge tremendously. Let us pursue scientific endeavour under an enlightened royal aegis! Let us turn England into a shining centre of science— the only source of understanding human nature!"

"We wish it were so straightforward," said the Queen. "A betterment of the human race is a grandiose task never attempted on that scale!"

They discussed the Club's report for a considerable time, Galton's plans being the focus of it. The Queen made a few very precise comments, from which it was clear that she was intrigued by particular notions regarding human body chemistry as the report made an example of Mr Dalton's colour-blindness as a hereditary deficiency. "You suggested," said the Queen, "that future advances of natural sciences would be able to correct this kind of problem. One would like to know, Mr Wells, what has your enlightened time achieved by the end of this century? You might know, gentlemen—it is not a secret—that our youngest son, Leopold, has a severe hereditary affliction—"

Alice knew that Prince Leopold, only a year her junior, was a sickly child. It was not widely publicized that Leopold had haemophilia—a debilitating blood condition of non-clotting, for which neither cure nor treatment existed. It was rumoured that the disease, which affected only boys, was inherited from their mother's side.[16]

Wells nodded gravely. "Your Majesty, we still have no treatment of this condition in the 1890s, but it might be coming; many scholars are working now to elucidate the mysterious mechanisms of heredity as well as nature of blood. My future time has many medical advances. Antiseptics—which must be broadly introduced across the nineteenth century—would save scores of life lost in surgeries, as in the Crimean campaign. Discovery of invisible infectious organisms by Mr Pasteur has completely changed medical science just in a few decades. Imagine what we could do if we exchange and introduce this knowledge across the century as far into the past as the Macchinetta can carry us!"

"Your Majesty!" said Dodgson resolutely. "We can make Oxford and Cambridge flourish beyond any dreams, enhanced with the accumulated impact of the best and the brightest from across the century. Please consider! We indeed might have a chance to change history—not through Napoleonic madness, but in a conscious and benevolent way—as we use the tools given to us for purposes of enlightenment!"

"Isn't it rather presumptious," said Lord Derby, shaking his head, "to think that history can be changed at will—by a mere human intervention short of magic? And one hardly believes in magic these days!"

"Mr Dodgson does!" thought Alice.

The Queen spoke. "It might never be possible to change Time," she said, "but if it were, would we not desire to attempt such a change in a rational, scientific way—as we change land and water, and all the natural elements bequeathed to us by the Creator? Isn't Time one of these elements—that River Times you describe so endearingly in your remarkable report?

"As the Dutch conquered their land from the sea, inch by inch over centuries—could we fashion levees to prevent dangerous floods on the River Times? Could we level its rapids and drain its marches? Could we build dams and dig channels?

"What do we know about this River? What sources feed it? Does it have any tributaries? Is it a steady, one-way flow, or a changeable multitude of small currents and eddies? How and why does it change its speed? Does it stay the same for all epochs and civilizations, or does it dry out in some but runs deep and clear in others?"

"Your Majesty!" said Wells. "It is my opinion—and Mr Dodgson, as a mathematician, might not agree—that the geometry they taught us at school is founded on a misconception, and there are really four dimensions, three which we call the three planes of space, and a fourth, Time.[17] The material nature of Time is not known—and that the Macchinetta is the first and the only experimental way to study it."

"Gentlemen!" said Queen rising from her seat. "We do not know if you will succeed—but if your Club wishes to attempt to improve the situation through that nearly magical device, we are not the one to stop you. Quite the opposite, we will help you—even as the waves of change sweep along the River Times! This activity will necessarily remain clandestine until time comes to make it public—and that may not be for years. We do not know how long the change will take. Prepare yourselves for a long and unrewarding labour. Your role is likely more important than any secret society's ever has been. It depends on Mr Wells and his little machine to test and show us what the future will be like and how it could change.

"Even with all the magnificent labour Englishmen have been involved in across the globe, on the seven seas—with everything that has been achieved in the last century—the world seems to be sliding back toward savagery.

"The Alice's Message, we believe, is true. We *can* feel its nonsense in our bones; we can feel senseless geological perturbances as if described by Mr Lyell's pen[18]—a *horror scenario!*[19] Alas, we *cannot* trust in the beneficial progress that Mr Darwin has promised to us in his great book. Human history does not seem to work this way—not by itself. To quote Mr Wells' report, 'the growing pile of civilization might happen to be only a foolish heaping that must inevitably fall back upon and destroy its makers in the end'![20]

"We should not wait for a future shock-wave that would pollute our time, pushing its fear and madness back against the flow of the River Times! We will try to steer the Ship of History, which seems to be going nowhere. And England will lead—as it has always done.

"Time seems to be seriously *out of joint*—and if we wish *to set it right*, let us make plans to save the world!"

CHAPTER VIII

Mr Dodgson Takes a Brief Continental Tour

*I*n March of 1867, encouraged by their successful recruitment of Lady Ada Lovelace, the Time Club renamed themselves the Time Corps. Lady Lovelace was their first recruit for what they hoped would become a veritable army of the best and brightest minds, in both theory and practice, from the civilized world across the entire Nineteenth Century.

Galton summarized his hopes, saying, "The Time Corps' most noble goal should be to identify a few hundred of the best scholars, inform them of our intentions, and work together to save humanity by altering the very course of history, thereby avoiding the inevitable catastrophic decline of civilization."

Dalton agreed and pleaded, "What are we going to do? Just sit around and wait while nonsense and silliness engulphs the entire world in even bloodier wars? Are we going to be content to just watch helplessly as future madness and incivility, like a filthy, putrid mass of industrial pollution comes backing up the River Times to kill and poison all of us? I'm neither ready nor willing to do that! Are you?"

"No!" the other members responded loudly, almost in unison.

Galton interjected. "I wonder if we might excuse Alice for a few minutes? I would like to propose a rather delicate idea that might not be appropriate for someone of such tender years."

Darwin looked at Alice. "Would you mind, Alice?" he asked. "For just a few minutes?"

Alice was disappointed, but did not show it. "Not at all." She left the room, closing the heavy study door behind her.

"I believe that we should encourage those scholars who join us to intermarry in order to create children of the highest intelligence! I call it 'viriculture'. I wrote a whole book on this subject."

"Nonsense!" Lady Lovelace declared. "I refuse to become involved in any such immoral and preposterous scheme that seeks to regulate human reproduction for the purpose of creating some sort of super-race! If you pursue this idea I will withdraw my membership in this group."

Darwin quickly intervened. "I agree with Lady Lovelace, Francis, that sort of thing would be inherently immoral. Let's avoid those sort of radical ideas and continue to investigate what we can do without offending people's sensitivities." Galton grumbled, but let the idea drop for the time being. "Lady Lovelace," Darwin continued, "would you please ask Alice to rejoin us?"

Lady Lovelace got up and went to find Alice. When she located her, she confided in Alice what Galton had suggested and then explained, "I am already married and I am not about to marry anyone else! I absolutely detest any plans to regulate human reproduction. I am quite happy with interbreeding animals to improve them for the common good, but that is my limit! And at any rate, almost all scholars are men and thus could not possibly marry and have children, even in Galton's fantastic plans!"

"Thank you for telling me about this," Alice replied. "I was a bit disappointed when they asked me to leave. However, what would be wrong if clever women chose, of their own free will, to marry clever men? Why should babies suffer from inheriting inferior brains? Mr Galton's ideas seem quite reasonable to me, as long as people weren't forced to do this."

"I agree with that in principle, but we should let nature take its own course. Besides it could not be easily implemented. People ordinarily have other reasons for getting married; saving civilization is not normally one of them! Come, they are probably awaiting our return."

When they reentered the study they found heated discussions underway about various practical and psychological issues with recruitment into the Time Corps from other decades. Not everyone that Wells had approached seemed able to believe in, much less confide in, a visitor from either the future or the past. Wells reported that some people even had trouble seeing and hearing him, as if their vision and hearing was unable to focus entirely on such a radical thing as a time traveller.

After several hours of deliberations the decision was made to organize a dozen trips back into time to determine how receptive people would be to the Corps' goals. With that plan of action the meeting was adjourned.

Dodgson's own travels on behalf of the Time Corps occurred in space, not time, when he visited Russia in 1867. This was quite a remarkable event for him, since it would be the only time he would ever leave the British Isles.

Alice was allowed to read Dodgson's amusing diary of his trip,[21] which included one month in Russia, from the 26th of July to the 28th of August. He had been accompanied by his Christ Church friend, the Reverend Henry Liddon, who was on a semi-official visit. Liddon carried a private letter from Samuel Wilberforce, the Bishop of Oxford,[22] to Philaret, the Metropolitan of Moscow.

Alice was amused by many of the funny notes in this Russian Journal, such as the following account, in an entry marked "July 26 (F[riday].)", of Dodgson and Liddon entering Russia on a train from Königsberg in Prussia to St Petersburg. Aboard, they met *an Englishman who had lived in Petersburg for 15 years, & was returning from a visit to Paris and London. He was most kind in answering our questions, ... but gave us rather dismal prospects of what is before us, as he says very few speak any language but Russian. As an instance of the extraordinary long words which the language contains, he spelt for me the following:* (Alice tried to read the Cyrillic letters but recognized only a few)

ЗАЩИЩАЮЩИХСЯ

which, written in English letters, is Zashtsheeshtshayou-shtsheekhsya:—this alarming word is a genitive plural of a participle, and means "of persons defending themselves..."

Alice laughed in disbelief. "The Classical Greek is easier!" she thought.

The journal was only a cover, of course, in case Russian secret police searched through traveller's belongings they would have to read lengthy and rather silly records of Mr Dodgson arguing with hotel servants and cab drivers in his broken Russian and listening to *"bewildering jabber of the natives"*, as he put it.

Dodgson's real goals were much more serious. His report to the Time Corps included three thick volumes with numerous charts and tables of an extremely technical nature. Alice understood very little of its chapters concerning Mathematical Foundations of Physics of Time and Space. She knew more about the Organic Chemistry of Extremely Long Molecules, which she was currently studying.

Dodgson's month in the enigmatic Eastern Orthodox Empire was spent in constant consultations with recruited naturalists and mathematicians. Alice could hardly pronounce the lengthy names of Russian scholars she saw in the report, such as Dmitri Ivanovich Mendeleev, the discoverer of the Periodic Table, and the mathematical genius Nikolai Ivanovich Lobachevsky, the founder of what they called the "Newest Geometry".

By that time, Dodgson was finally convinced to renounce his faithful allegiance to the Fifth Postulate of Euclid. One of his goals in Russia was to examine the hidden archives of Lobachevsky, who had challenged Euclidean geometry. The Time Corps had recruited Lobachevsky by travelling back in time to 1829, immediately after he become well-known for his seminal paper. He had died in 1856, unrecognized by his contemporaries, and had asked the Time Corps to retrieve his cache of archives containing important unpublished notes. Dodgson obtained those from an undercover Corps agent at the annual Russian country fair (*yarmarka*) in Nizhny Novgorod on Volga River, which he and Liddon had visited in August.

One of the setbacks was that they had not yet made contact with János Bolyai in Transylvania, another mathematical genius who had, independently from Lobachevsky, discovered non-Euclidean geometry. Bolyai had died insane and unrecognized in 1860.

"Out of nothing I have created a strange new universe," wrote Bolyai, who well understood what he had done. Time travel to Transylvania in the 1820s, which Wells and Galton had attempted, proved to be unsuccessful. This was the time of Metternich's police state, and progress of science in Hungary was slow (the Academy of Science there was established only in 1825, with the help of the young Count Széchenyi, whom Dalton secretly recruited during his visit to England). The Time Corps was unable to retrieve Bolyai's enormous archive. They only managed to find out that the 14,000 pages had been seized by the local governor, who suspected that it contained military secrets, and that it was probably rotting in some medieval-era cellar.

In Alice's own time, they had also suffered the tragic loss of another mathematician, Bernhard Riemann in Göttingen, who had died in 1866, aged only thirty-nine. The Corps monitored and nurtured Herr Riemann's early career. At the age of twenty-six, Riemann outlined his vision of a mathematics of many different kinds of space—only one of which was our own, flat Euclidean space! Riemann's "elliptic geometry" changed everything about how we view the world.

The work of those brilliant mathematicians—Bolyai, Lobachevsky, and Riemann[23]—was especially important for the Time Corps. Their amazing insights into the Geometry of Space and Time had the potential to lead to the coveted knowledge on the mechanics of time-travel and time-communication, and perhaps might even explain the construction of the Macchinetta. Who knows how many other scholars would die unknown and unrecognized over the century?

Travelling in Russia in the summer 1867, Dodgson had carefully impersonated an absent-minded Englishman. The travel was not completely safe or comfortable. The Crimean

War fought by the two Empires—the first and the *only* military conflict they had had in centuries—had ended eleven years ago with the British and their allies victorious, leaving the Russians quite apprehensive toward England. Consequently, Dodgson's clandestine meetings with Russian scholars would have been construed as spying, which, Alice thought, it *was* indeed.

Alice knew that Dodgson had visited a number of inventors and ingenious technicians, talking and taking notes on all matters of science and technology. Notes, of which many survive to our day, and can be seen on a permanent exhibit in the Crystal Palace, were written with India ink on thin silk handkerchiefs imported from China. (Dodgson had purchased many of those handkerchiefs at that fair in Nizhny Novgorod, and employed them for the purpose of time travel.)

Imperial Russia appeared in Dodgson's travelogue as a rather alien, Oriental country with devout Orthodox priests and monks, somewhat resembling a medieval Byzantine Empire. The vast capital of St Petersburg amazed him: *"we walked here and there about this marvellous city. It is so utterly unlike anything I have ever seen, that I feel as if I could and should be content to do nothing for many days but roam about it."* Alice knew, however, that he devoted his time to much more than roaming the improbable city built by French and Italian architects, and admiring its many churches, or taking a visit to Peterhof summer palace by steamer—*"down the tideless, saltless Gulf of Finland."*

The diary said nothing about the visit to the Imperial St Petersburg University, with its beautiful buildings overlooking the wide Neva River, where Dodgson called on Dmitri Ivanovich Mendeleev who was a Professor there. The future great chemist, then only thirty-four, was working on mixtures of alcohol and water, not knowing that he will be recruited by Wells in 1898. However, Mendeleev's younger self had to be informed about it, which was the standard Corps practice. Alice knew that the younger Dmitri gladly approved, and the clandestine meetings had already produced highly valuable results—the Periodic Table will be coming in 1869!

A quite different Russian visionary, who would also become famous later, lived at that time just a short distance from Mendeleev's University building. His literary characters roamed the same wide St Petersburg streets in a very depressed mood. He had one of those names that Alice could hardly read: Fyodor Mikhailovich Dostoevsky. Many acknowledged that he was the best in exposing the enigmatic Russian soul. Dodgson, however, was not able to meet Dostoevsky, who had departed for a trip to Europe with his new wife in April 1867 while his latest novel, *Crime and Punishment,* published in 1866, was still being much talked about. Unfortunately, the novel had not yet been translated into foreign languages. Curious about him, Alice had asked Wells about Dostoevsky's work and he had told her a lot about the fascinating and alarming Russian literature of the 1870s–1890s.

As Wells rather sharply put it, Fyodor Mikhailovich "devised a sort of mystical imperialism based on the idea of Holy Russia and her mission—where the *muzhik* was supposed to worship and revere his Tsar and to love to serve a gentleman."[24]

"Why then," thought Alice, "would Raskolnikov, his student, put forward his ghastly 'Napoleonic' idea of murder serving the higher purpose? And furthermore, why would they, in the future, put the blame for that on Mr Darwin? *'It is wrong from beginning to end.'*"

On his departure from Russia by way of Warsaw, Dodgson noted:—

"AUG. 28 (W[ednesday].) *We spent the day in wandering about Warsaw.... The town, as a whole, is one of the noisiest and dirtiest I have yet visited.*"

He wrote nothing about the latest Polish uprising of freedom-fighters that was cruelly suppressed here in 1863. Neither did his journal mention anything about the sweeping reforms of 1861 that had been implemented by Tsar Alexander II. Only a short time ago, in April 1866, a student named Dmitri Karakozov had tried to assassinate this reformer Tsar! All of that was so different from recent English history, and quite like the ominous vision from a vague, distant future, as if it had been described by Dostoevsky!

Alice wondered if a timeline can be drastically changed by a single-handed attempt like Karakozov's—or Raskolnikov's. What could bear more weight on history's scale? The enormous, gradual work on civilizing reforms, or a single deranged youth, positioned with his pistol in the right place, at an opportune time?

In October of 1867, Darwin called a meeting of the Time Corps to listen to a status report of their expeditions. Once the meeting commenced, Wells began. "Most scholars of the 1820s to the 1850s that were contacted had open minds, or perhaps they were simply more naïve. They readily embraced such an amazing opportunity to work with future colleagues. Conversely, many of those from the 1870s and 80s were more jaded and less willing to share ther inventions and ideas with the past. They argued that any tampering with history, no matter how seemingly slight, might alter the future in ways that might negatively affect their own original timeline events. One man was very concerned that he might not even have met his wife and would not have experienced the joy of having his own children! Some had visions of great wealth resulting from their discoveries and efforts, and didn't want to jeopardize that possibility. Who knows? Perhaps they're right.

"Logistics will be a serious difficulty for some willing associates. Many recruits will have to work from their own time, since they could not just disappear for a long period to visit the 1860s. Even those who might be able to convince their families that they are taking a business trip to some remote location like Canada will still be under danger of their secret mission being discovered. Very few said that they might be willing to emigrate to the future, and live there under an assumed name. Understandably, some have families that they don't want to just abandon. There were more of those that wanted to escape to the past, mainly to the time of their own youth, mysteriously vanishing from their own time, and assuming another persona."

Darwin interjected. "We could help some of them to relocate, though I personally don't approve of such escapism. We will inevitably damage families by such a sudden loss. It isn't fair to any of them!"

"Some events could be tragic," admitted Galton. "However, they might be an enormous blessing to tens of thousands or even millions if doing so results in averting a war. We would have to be willing to sacrifice the few for the possibility of benefitting future multitudes. No one said this would be painless or easy."

Wells continued. "Look, I'm exhausted and I've been under enormous stress for the past year, since I'm the only one who can pilot the Macchinetta. For some reason that I don't understand, the device simply wo'n't work without me and my role has largely evolved into shuttling people around, one passenger at a time. Further, I'm the one who is doing most of the recruiting, since my name isn't known to anyone before the 1890s. It wouldn't be reasonable to send Charles Darwin a decade backward or forward, since he is well-known to everyone, and his appearance as an older or younger man would no doubt cause unnecessary problems.

"Recruitment into the Time Corps network from the *contemporary* body of scholars alive now in 1867 hasn't been straightforward either, although we can travel freely within our own time. Strict secrecy must necessarily surround all of our enterprise, although the Queen and a few of her ministers know about our activities. The Crown has already provided discreet financial help and we hope that they will continue to do so over the years. Identified candidates have been approached, Freemason-style, after a thorough process of selection based on their former and future performance. My cousin Charles, with his worldwide authority and expansive network of more than one thousand corre-spondents in all fields of natural sciences, has helped to identify many and we are hopeful that many will join us. However, not everyone—whether in the past, present, and future—can be taken into our confidence. Not everyone will be open to our radical idea and plans. Some have already plainly told us that they don't believe time travellers and have angrily dismissed us as raving lunatics or crazy inventor-fanatics, shrugging us off, even alerting authorities when espionage was suspected. A few cases have unfortu-nately even led to conflict, especially in some foreign countries. Language barriers haven't helped, especially in Germany and France. Some contactees have been plainly suspicious of an Englishman who has declared himself quite seriously as having coming from the future. Probably quite a few rumours have been created by our activities.

"A huge and unexpected problem, as you well know, has been how to transfer information. We cannot carry printed books, scholarly papers, manuscripts, or even any hand notes; nothing written or printed on paper! In my first attempts to ride the Macchinetta, all of my cotton-based clothing, to my embarassment, dissolved within a few minutes. Apparently, there is some emanation in the time flow that acts as an acid upon *cellulose*, the plant fiber. Now we must dress only in animal textiles—wool or silk or leather. Tweeds work just fine. Very annoying, however, is that no paper can withstand the corrosive effects of time travel! It crumbles as if burnt and rapidly turns into fine, cold ashes that are scattered on the River Times."

Dodgson jokingly interrupted, "Perhaps we should revert to the time-tested clay tablets of Nineveh!"[25]

Wells laughed. "Well, first we tried to write on parchment,[26] but that was costing us a small fortune, and had to be clandesinely commissioned from friendly craftsmen. With the help of an American inventor, one Mr Pratt of Alabama, the Time Corps managed to develop an ingenious 'Type Writing Machine'[27] that we now use to produce a decent print on expensive parchment and silk sheets. Those silk handkerchiefs that Mr Dodgson used in Russia serve quite well!

"We finally realized that photographic glass plates could be carried across time. However, transportation of photographic apparatuses across time was less easy. I have brought over some portable ones, even a hand-held camera from the 1890s, but in my time most photographers had switched to flexible, celluloid film coated with an emulsion. This is of no use, since cellulose-based film crumbled just like paper when taken downtime! One of the best photographers of the 1860s is, fortuitously, our Mr Charles Dodgson, and his improvements of glass-plate techniques made things a bit easier."

Wells' discussion continued for three hours on similar topics and issues.

The Code of Life

*A*s the Time Corps met again a fortnight later, only four of them were present: Darwin, Galton, Dalton, and Dodgson. Alice was invited and expected to arrive soon. Wells was engaged elsewhere, or, as they learned to say, *elsewhen*.

"I keep thinking that Alice—I can speak freely while she is not here—has been changed by her message in many ways," said Dodgson. "For instance, her childhood attraction to barnacles has changed into a fast and perfectly professional interest this very summer. Was it by chance?"

"A passion in natural history is perfectly normal in a child," shrugged Darwin, "and an animal group of choice is often due to early impressions. Alice told me about her seaside excursions observing the common *Balanus* at the Welsh coast as a small child. I myself took an interest in beetles at a very young age. Oh, I was such a zealous collector!" He chuckled. "Once I saw two beetles and seized one in each hand; then I saw a third and new kind, which I could not bear to lose, so that I popped the one I held into my right hand into my mouth. Alas! It ejected some intensely acrid fluid, which burnt my tongue so that I was forced to spit the beetle out, which was lost.[28] Such a passion for collecting is clearly innate, although none of my sisters or brother ever had it. One grows up to be a specialist in a certain zoological group—be it butterflies, beetles, or scorpions."

"But Alice wasn't interested in beetles or scorpions," insisted Dodgson. "Of all bizarre creatures, she was specifically focused on barnacles, and that led her directly to you, since you are the world-known expert!"

"Well, I definitely used to be that, though no longer," admitted Darwin. "I spent eight years intensely working on Cirripedia between 1845 and 1854, with four monographic volumes published in 1851–54."

"But exactly at that time—in 1852—Alice was born!" exclaimed Dodgson.

"Yes, and already as a very small child she expressed her interest!" noted Galton. "She told me she was first taken to Anglesey in 1857, at age five. Incidentally, Anglesey was a sacred island of the Druids! Could this be a connection, an influence that eventually brought the two of you together? And soon, in 1866, Wells conveniently found the best anchorage for his Macchinetta here in Down."

"It is as if some future observer was casting his lines or nets in the River Times to capture a sensitive recipient—indeed, a medium!" said Dodgson. "Barnacles could have served as bait; an image impressed on a brilliant, receptive child's brain, so that she would grow up and find your home, and thus be brought together with you and Wells."

"Yes, it is quite plausible that these future messages could reinforce Alice's interest in marine biology," Darwin agreed. "A sea-creature theme in this Wonderland text is very powerful. The rabbit-hole leads to a purely terrestrial underground kingdom—unless one counts the Pool of Tears—but some very strange aquatic organisms appear from nowhere in Wonderland."

"Yes, the odd pair of the Gryphon and the Mock Turtle appear suddenly, as if out of thin air," admitted Dodgson. "Both claim to have attended an underwater school. We have already discussed them many times, and agreed that they could possibly signify some facets of a future educational crisis."

"Now I can see even more significance!" exclaimed Darwin. "Perhaps Earth's climate may be disturbed by a comet or some other astronomical cause. An Underwater School might indicate rising sea levels in the future! Another flood may be coming! But this time there will be no rescuing ark and no Ararat on which to land. Humankind may be forced to relocate to the sea bottom and become aquatic! This type of global catastrophe could happen if the Arctic and Antarctic ice fields were to melt. It has happened before, as sedimentary geology shows us. As giant seas encroach on vast continents, coastal cities would be submerged, creating a true New Atlantis!"

"The Message text, as always, does not allow such a direct interpretation," complained Dodgson. "Babbage and his Time Corps technicians went through it numerous times with the Analytical Engine, but it is very hard to make sense out of most this text's nonsense."

"Be that as it may," said Galton, "the question still remains; *how* does such an influence work and persist? What is the physical mechanism of this mysterious magnetism that alters one's desires and passions, predestines one's professional interests, and brings together three very unlikely people right here at Down?"

"In the Time Corps, the best minds are still very far from understanding the complex chemistry of the brain and sensory organs," said Darwin. "We do not know how the mind forms its images, and what influences the alien emanations might have."

"I know very little of chemistry," said Dodgson to Dalton, "but I enjoy constant exchanges with you and your modern followers. And meeting Dmitri Ivanovich in Russia put my mind on a quite new track. I think we have been advancing quite a bit into the structure of molecules. What attracts me is a possibility that there is indeed a numerical, Pythagorean, numerical Language of Life embedded right here in our bodies, in our cells. Such a mathematical and cellular language could possibly account for all properties of life."

"Are you talking about my 'provisional hypothesis' of pangenesis—a model of how heredity works?"[29] asked Darwin. "The biologists so far have not come close to the chemical structure of pangenetic *gemmules*, the universal hereditary particles I posited. Francis did some experiments on what he calls blood-heredity, and was rather disappointed in his results."

"I would not be surprised," said Dodgson, "if all necessary instructions for Life are indeed encoded! Language is the most powerful tool of man, so why could not Nature have an intricate language of her own?"

"In a poetical sense, yes," shrugged Darwin, "but what would it use to write it with, and on what?"

"On molecules of course!" exclaimed Dalton. "On, in, with, and by chemicals as yet undiscovered, which would house and hide mysterious messages inside them, as if written in some kind of code in charge of heredity—to be read and deciphered by other molecules."

"Life and Mind are the most complex things in the world, and their features are inherited from parents to children," said Galton pensively. "It seems quite logical that their language should be imprinted on the living molecules—just like

Alice's sensory receptors received and decoded the alien message."

"An interesting idea," smiled Darwin, "but one wouldn't be able to write much using carbon, nitrogen, and oxygen atoms—and living bodies are made mainly of these light chemical elements."

"Perhaps not with atoms themselves," insisted Dodgson, "but with their combinations one probably can. I spent years designing all kinds of secret codes and letter games—believe me, the possibilities are almost endless!" He smiled. "As in my simple game of *Doublets* that I showed you before, my modest invention that amuses children and adults equally. For instance, 'RAT' to 'RAG' to 'TAG' to 'TAR', a simple permutation series of three-letter words. Why, our alphabet has only twenty-six letters—and that is enough to write all of the Scriptures, and all of Shakespeare!"

"And all the modern newspaper poppycock that quadruples every year!" chuckled Dalton. "And, by the way, you can just reverse 'RAT' into 'TAR'."

"Or anagram both into 'ART'," noted Galton.

"On a more serious note," said Dalton, "our Time Corps associates just discovered a physician in Basel, one Dr Friedrich Miescher, a contemporary of yours.[30] He found an incredibly long molecule in cell nucleus that he called *nuclein*. It is a type of heavy acid, loaded with phosphorus, which is very unusual. My experts from across the century advise that we test it in our biological experiments, in addition to many wonderful proteinous molecules—"

The conversation was interrupted by Alice entering with a stack of mail. One of her gladly accepted chores in recent months was helping Darwin to sort his correspondence. A lot of it was concerning the Time Corps business, but there was a huge backlog of research publications sent to the great scientist from all over the civilized world. Alice's knowledge of German was quite valuable; so much scholarly literature on the Continent was written in this language, which Darwin readily admitted he was not well versed in.

"Mr Darwin," Alice said to their host, "could you please look at that reprint that came in the post last winter? Its pages were never cut. I allowed myself to cut them, since this paper was about plant breeding. Mr Galton told me specifically to look for the reports on breeding simple alternative traits, and that one, in addition, has an incredible amount of experimental data!"

"It is in German," said Darwin, taking a thin brochure from Alice's hands. "The title is just 'Versuche über Pflanzenhybriden'—'Studies on Plant Hybridization'—"

"I made a digest for you," said Alice. "The reprint is from a local Natural Sciences Society—*Verhandlungen des natur-forschenden Vereines in Brünn,* Vol. 4 for 1866. Where is Brünn?"

"A capital of Moravia," Darwin replied.

"And where is Moravia?" asked Alice.

"Next to Bohemia, of course! They both are parts of the Austrian Empire," explained Dodgson who liked maps.

"Are these parts as remote as Transylvania?" asked Alice, quite mindful of their failure, within those backwater Habsburg possessions, to engage János Bolyai into the Time Corps activities.

"No, Moravia is much more civilized," said Darwin. "There was a keen gentleman in Brünn who died about twenty years ago—an aristocrat who was not only breeding sheep, but also carefully studied their heredity. He bought some very expensive Merino stock in England. His name was Count Imre Festetics, though I am not sure that I have pronounced it correctly."[31]

"I have a feeling that we need to contact the author of this paper," said Galton, who was looking through a rather dense

German text brought by Alice. "His hybridization results are solid. He has some remarkable statistics, and he uses a very interesting system of notation. And, after all, he is our contemporary; what a relief, we can simply write a letter to him!"

Alice smiled: "Yes, and we can write him a real letter—not on that silly parchment we use for time-travel notes, but on good old postal paper! I will see how much postage is needed to go to Brünn."

"What was the author's name?" inquired Darwin.

"Gregor Mendel," Alice replied.

So it happened that their newest recruit was brought from Brünn to London, and placed to work with Darwin's friend Joseph Hooker in the Royal Kew Gardens, the world's finest botanical institution. His story is well known to everyone now, since the hidden archives of the illustrious Time Corps are finally being made public. Not a Lobachevsky perhaps, but definitely a Euclid of his trade, this modest Augustinian friar breeding peas in his abbey's front garden, without even a greenhouse—had single-handedly discovered the Rules of Heredity. Brother Gregor was a natural statistician, and bred his pea plants to resolve a simple rule: parents' characteristics do not blend in children, but exist as temporary combinations. Out of study of these combinations—or, better to say, combinations of Darwin's *gemmules*, those precious particles carrying the right Nuclein,—our entire Science of Heredity sprang forth. It was exactly the obscure talents like Mendel's that the Time Corps was searching for! With only two years of education at the University of Vienna, snubbed by the academic establishment, without any sponsors or scholarly credentials, his work would very likely have been forgotten—as was that of dozens and hundreds of unknown talents.

By a strange coincidence—or a mysterious influence from the future?—Gregor Mendel had visited London in 1862, the Year of Alice's First Message as it is called today. We do not know why the Augustinian did not call on Darwin then. Perhaps he had not read the *Origin of Species* yet; the book had been translated into German in 1860, but in Mendel's library we find only its second edition of 1863, with many notes on the margins. Most likely, Mendel was just being shy and did not want to impose himself on the famous naturalist. Instead, he went to the Great London Exposition, where he could see unfinished parts of Babbage's Analytical Engine, among other things.[32]

One thing is clear: if Mendel's discovery hadn't been made known to Darwin and the Time Corps in 1867—that is, if Alice had not touched that reprint from the *Verhandlungen des naturforschenden Vereines in Brünn*, and if it had remained uncut in Darwin's library[33]—the amazing developments in natural science of the 19th century would have been set back by decades.

The Code of Life would never have been deciphered by the mid-1870s, and the Engineering of Heredity wouldn't become a reality by the 1890s, when the structure of Friedrich Miescher's Nuclein was decoded completely, with its remarkable billions of units per each and every human cell.

Colour-blindness—and, what was much more important, the debilitating haemophilia—would not have been effectively cured (by insertion of correctly re-phrased Nuclein codes into the cell's gemmules) by 1902. To think that the heir to the Russian throne could die young from this inherited blood condition! He would not have become the future Tsar Alexci II the Just, who would peacefully rule as a constitutional monarch from 1937 to 1991. (Unfortunately, his mother's uncle Leopold, Duke of Albany, did not live to see the cure. Neither did Leopold's mother, Queen Victoria, who died in 1901.)

Many other accounts of medical advance brought by Gemmule Therapy made the golden pages of ensuing history of the betterment of the human race since then. Numerous molecules have been found and successfully applied to ensure intelligence, civility, and moral strength—and to curb base, brutish instincts that contributed so much to all the past suffering of humankind.

This is how, in a changed timeline, the Victorian Civilization reached the *fin de siècle* and passed into the Glorious Twentieth Century. And to think that all these marvellous events happened just within a few years!

Alice, meanwhile, took her modest part in those developments as a Natural Science student at Lady Muriel Hall, a college of the Academia Hypatiana. This new female-only university was introduced on the Queen's suggestion, and half-heartedly approved by Parliament in 1869.

Dean Liddell had mixed feelings about his daughter's desire to become a Heredity Engineer, but admitted that this had all started with barnacles, years ago. "Times a-changing," he famously said. "Young ladies can now have a college education—albeit these girl colleges surely ought to pay full attention to home economy—and the Classics."

All this, of course, was still in the future when, in 1867, Alice was first reading Mendel's "Versuche über Pflanzen-hybriden." She was at the same time keenly interested in old Dalton's ideas on what he called the Code of Life—how those longest and diverse molecules—a protein, or a Nuclein—are built, and how they could be possibly altered by certain kinds of chemicals and emanations.

Alice was impressed and humbled by all the changes that happened in the close-knit world of scholars that now existed around her, many active in Oxford just next door to her father's college.

So far, very few of these new discoveries and inventions, as well as of those brought by Wells and the future scholars, had yet penetrated into the general public. The Time Corps was very careful—and managed so far—not to release any novel information coming from future decades that would lead to weaponry improvement, whether domestic or abroad. The progress on disarmament was frustratingly slow!

By the end of 1867, Darwin's spacious house, where he was to spend the last decades of his life working incessantly for the Time Corps, was already transformed into The Corps headquarters. Its greenhouses, with a team of skilled gardeners, allowed all kinds of work in plant hybridization and heredity. The adjacent facilities for cell biology studies were stocked with the finest microscopes, commissioned from German and Dutch craftsmen.

John Dalton's mood also hadn't improved lately, as he kept obtaining from Wells and other researchers new reports on the late 1890s.

"Too much emphasis on weaponry—just too much!" Dalton grumbled as he reviewed heaps of parchments with digests of future chemistry achievements. "Smokeless gunpowder compositions, propellants, and gases—all kinds of gases, some very toxic. Mendeleev himself is working on new gunpowder with a hefty commission from the Russian Navy!"

"I talked to him personally upon your request," said Wells. "Dmitri assures me that he is largely a theoretician interested in low pressures. He uses their War Ministry money for gunpowder development," Wells chuckled, "while his scholarly interest lies, he says, at the other end of the gun."

"Well," said Dalton, unimpressed, "too many are working on the gun's business end. But you told us that Queen Victoria's reign is still very stable in 1899; that's good, we need stability. We do not wish a major tectonic event such as the French Revolution!"

"Yes, if we are to change human history in the same way as natural objects change," said Galton, "we'll achieve it only by *small increments,*" he winked at Darwin.

The great naturalist nodded quite seriously. "Yes, this is what I have proposed to be the mechanism of evolution," he said. "*Natura non facit saltus.* Natural selection always acts very slowly, often only at long intervals of time, and generally on a very few of the inhabitants of the same region at the same time."[34]

Francis Galton smiled as he recognized the passage; in fact, he knew most of his cousin's great 1859 book by heart.

"I wonder," he thought, "which book would future generations value and preserve the most—the *Origin of Species* or *Alice's Adventures*? What would they opt for to guide their lives? A deep and rewarding knowledge of discovery in natural history, which we all cherish and praise today—or mindless language games to amuse them in a little time they would spare from slaving at senseless office jobs? I guess it depends on what *we* will achieve, here and now, and across the nineteenth century!"

M r   W e l l s   G i v e s   E v i d e n c e

An urgent meeting was called by Wells for the 14th of December 1867, almost two years after Alice had been introduced to the fearless time traveller and his Macchinetta. Alice, Wells, Dodgson, Dalton, and Galton arrived at Darwin's home and seated themselves in his study. Wells produced a heavy stack of glass plates and a bundle of parchments from a leather portfolio. Visibly disturbed, he paced around the study for a few minutes, then finally said, "I've brought some evidence that things are changing at the end of the century. Whether this is due to our efforts or not, I don't know. These changes are strange and disturbing. There are three major things that are not the same as they were last time. They changed abruptly. The first and the most shocking for me is that my own life has changed drastically!"

"How?" exclaimed Darwin, who always argued for very small, incremental and very gradual, evolutionary changes. "Are you all right?"

Wells smiled weakly. "Physically, yes. Mentally, I don't know; what happened is very odd. In my diary, I have always carefully noted all my travels with the Macchinetta. This year, I managed to make over 60 substantial trips, mainly within the thirty-two years separating your and my time, but fewer to your past with Dalton and a few others. Your current time, 1867, is about an hour's journey from mine, which is currently 1899.

"I logged a total over three hundred hours on the River Times and I have been many days away from my home. As you know, the Macchinetta does not allow one to return into exactly the same moment from which one departed. If I were absent for two days, I would return two days later, and would usually have to explain my absence to someone, even though I have no family of my own and lead a rather flexible lifestyle being a free-lance journalist. It was usually rather easy for me to melt away.

"On my last recorded trip, a week ago, I returned to my home on the banks of the great River Times, but to my utter dismay, I slowly realized that I was not the same person! Or, more accurately, I was physically the same and still was an H. G. Wells, but my life and career had changed completely. I have a wife named Catherine!"

"But how do you feel?" asked Dodgson, amazed. "Is your mind split into your previous and current personae?"

"Not at all! The two are currently mingled and I retain both sets of memories; but they are starting to fuse dimly into one. I clearly remember everything I did in my time travels, but I think I am gradually losing the memory of my previous, different life in my own time. It is as if I woke up and still very vividly remembered a dream, and then it started fading slowly away. Everyone around me behaves as if nothing has happened!

"I don't think that I ever told you about my humble beginnings. My family, here at Bromley, was—is—far from being rich. Now in 1867, with me as their newborn, fourth son, they are struggling. I was employed as a free-lance journalist after I graduated from the University, but I never pursued a scholarly career. I was fortunate to be able to study for a year under the old man, Thomas Huxley; your good friend, Darwin."

"I am glad to learn that Huxley will be well and active in his advanced age," smiled Darwin.

"A great man! I learned a lot from him. As far as I can tell, all of my early background remained the same until 1890, the year when I was awarded my Bachelor's degree, but after that things began to change dramatically compared to what I remember. I have a feeling that the shift could have started with a short story which—in this new reality—I had written as a young man in 1888, at age twenty-two. I do not recall that in my previous lifetime having written anything of the sort!"

"What was this story about?" asked Alice.

Wells hesitated. "Time travel."

Everyone was stunned.

"It was titled *The Chronic Argonauts*,"[35] continued Wells, "and contained a rather brief narrative about a strangely named inventor, Dr Moses Nebogipfel. He builds a time machine, and is attacked by a mob in the normally peaceful Welsh town of Llyddwdd."

"I am unaware that time travel was ever depicted in a fictional story," said Dodgson. "Yours should have been the first."[36]

"It has been done, but rarely." admitted Wells. "After all, the subject is rather exotic. Naturally, most Utopian writing has been set in future. The concept of a time-traversing vehicle, however, was probably a completely novel idea that came to me—or rather to that version of me who wrote it in 1888 in this new, changed timeline. But this is not the most astonishing part.

"I am now famous! In the 1899 timeline I now come from, I find myself an accomplished writer in a very new genre. I seem to be the sole founder and artist in this style. Over the course of the last four years, I have produced several short novels, which became enormously popular. I even get a considerable profit from selling my books."

"What are they about?" inquired Alice who was listening very intently.

"Science," said Wells.

Darwin did not understand. "But how does one write novels about science? It is a dry and lonely pursuit; we scholars love it, but there is no romance in it. No one will read such a book!"

"Well, our grandfather Erasmus wrote a very long poem *The Loves of the Plants* about plant reproduction, which was quite amusing at his time," noted Galton.

"Mrs Shelley wrote her *Frankenstein* about a scientist—a rather mad one," offered Alice. How many times over the last months did her thoughts turn back to that book! She kept it close on her book-shelf at home, along with Dodgson's ear-marked volume, defaced by many a scribble and algebra-like notations. Alice tried her hand again and again at decoding the Future Message, as did many teams in the Time Corps, tirelessly scanning the text for hidden, Cabbalistic patterns.

Wells looked at them grimly. "Yes! They call my novels 'scientific romances'.[37] I wish I could bring some to show to you right now—but so far they only exist on paper. It would take weeks to hand-copy them onto parchment or to photograph page by page and carry those images on glass plates.

"These fantasies are very good! They are vivid, passionate, brightly animated narrations that create a hypnotic effect—not unlike Alice's Message. Some are about mad scientists like Mrs Shelley's—a vivisectionist making beasts into men; an anarchist student who makes himself invisible. The latest one is about vile creatures from Mars—a non-human species!—which try to conquer our world.

"But wait until you hear what the first one was called, one which I produced—in this new timeline—in 1895, and which gave me instant fame. It is titled—" Wells waited to create the suspense and announced with a flourish but rather sadly: "—*THE TIME MACHINE!*"

The announcement caught Alice as unawares as a thunder in the midst of a bright day. She felt she was inside a nightmare, flying high with autumn leaves through a cold gale. She was hardly able to listen to the ensuing flurry of questions and answers. Wells had to tell everyone at length what the book is about, and they all admired his bold visions of this uncommon writing. The Time Traveller described in the book (he had no name) has travelled far and saw a very disturbing future.

"It is a very smart little book," concluded Wells. "It was an immediate success in 1895. Honestly, I would not think I am—or was—or will be able to write like that."

They were all silent for a while, and then suddenly Dodgson spoke: "Do you think that could be another influence? What if, somehow, the ideas and outlandish characters of these 'science romances' were coming down to you in your new 1890s from the same source that sent the 1862 and 1863 texts to Alice in Oxford?"

Wells nodded. "Quite possible. I did not think about it! But the very moment I started to use the Macchinetta—which is very different from that fictional Time Machine, by the way—some change had already begun. I believe that we must have disturbed some part of the time flow. An earthwork of sorts; a dam was being created that forced the River Times to change course along a new bed."

"But you mentioned that you found evidence of other changes in 1899!" said Francis Galton. "I beg you, let us hear about them; try to remember what else changed, while you still can distinguish between your memories. Once your old memories fade, we will have no way to recover your previous timeline!"

"Yes," Wells nodded. "There is some rather good—albeit puzzling—news in foreign affairs. In Holland, the Hague Peace Conference has just opened in May—for the first time in history!"[38]

"It seems that the Time Corps efforts have somehow worked!" exclaimed Darwin.

"I'm not sure," replied Wells. "The Conference was initiated in 1898 by the new Russian Tsar. His name is Nicholas II."

"Please brief me on that royal person, as I am not well familiar with those future Romanovs of your time," said Dalton.

Wells smiled: "That *is* the change! *There was no Tsar by this name in my time.* Tsar Alexander III—who inherited the Romanov throne after his father was assassinated by terrorists in 1881—was still going strong in 1899, not yet sixty, and a vigorous giant of a man, in great health. I know that for sure!"

"Was he our ally?" asked Alice.

"Far from that!" said Wells. "His Majesty was rather xenophobic, and did not move much toward Britain or Europe. He was the Tsar who said 'Russia has only two allies: its Army and its Navy.' His father's reforms were effectively halted."

"Sounds rather reactionary," noted Dodgson. "That's a great change—a regressive one!—compared to Russia of Alexander II which I just visited a month ago. Today, in 1867, it seems to be quite on the road to progress! They are implementing civilizing reforms. And you just said, Alexander II—the reformer who freed their slaves—will be assassinated! This is *very* disturbing indeed! Are we to repeat the pattern of regicides and revolutions over and over?"

"In my new, altered timeline, Alexander III suddenly died five years ago, in 1894." continued Wells. "His son who took the throne was only twenty-six, and ill prepared to rule. Still, his initiative on disarmament is remarkable, and, he is married to our Queen's granddaughter, Alix. She is a daughter of Princess Alice, Grand Duchess of Hesse, and will be born in 1872."

"Interesting!" said Galton. "We need to recruit some royals to the Time Corps! This Nicholas II sounds as though he was born into new generation of softer, wiser rulers. Could it be that our work is already producing results?"

"I brought back some notes that could help," said Wells as he was unwrapping glass plates that had to be viewed in a special apparatus that he had brought along with him to the meeting. He flashed several names and faces on a wall.

"Here is this new Russian Tsar, Nicholas II, born in 1868. He is only thirty-one, two years younger than me."

"He indeed looks soft," agreed Darwin. "Well, hopefully he will not repeat the dire errors of his great-grandfather, the first Nicholas, whose reign ended in 1855 with the Crimean defeat and the Tsar's mysterious death."

"This Crimea is a special place," noted Galton, "perhaps one of those 'thin spots' where the fabric of time-space is especially vulnerable and prone to changes. Now I think that your meeting and rescuing Count Tolstoy there, Wells, might not have been a chance! And the place is so beautiful—a wild version of the Riviera! The Ancient Greeks owned it, the Genovese, and then the Tartars. Who would think that her Majesty's soldiers would fight the Russians on behalf of the Sultan there?"

The exotic names of Balaklava and Sevastopol were now known to every school-child, thought Alice as she recalled Mr Tennyson's voice when he read his famous patriotic lines about the Crimean War:

> *"Boldly they rode and well,*
> *Into the jaws of Death,*
> *Into the mouth of Hell*
> *Rode the six hundred."*

"Wait a moment—did you say this new Tsar of theirs was born in 1868?" Dalton asked in astonishment. They had never have seen the old polymath so agitated. He turned to Galton. "Do you think that his birth could be an effect of the Macchinetta?"

"Yes, I do!" replied Galton. *"Post hoc, ergo propter hoc.* I long suspected that the Macchinetta itself could serve as a magnetic device directly influencing heredity within the years it visits. And Wells lingered mostly here in 1866 and 1867. Wells—we'll need you to go back to 1899 and take a good look at young men and women born in and after these years!"

"Then, it might well be," said Dodgson in excitement, "that the 1860s are indeed the pivotal point in history—directly influencing the human race by changing hereditary codes!"

"There must be more, many more of those new children of the late 1860s and early 1870s, whose talents have not yet shown themselves by 1899!" exclaimed Darwin. "For all we know, there could be a young lawyer in South Africa or an obscure bicycle shop owner in rural Ohio born within these years, who will further change the course of history."

"There may also be some whose talents are revealed already!" said Wells. "A remarkable lady chemist of my age, born in Russian Poland, is working in Paris now—I mean in 1899. Her name is Marie Skłodowska Curie. She discovered a new chemical element they called radium—which exhibits some amazing properties the French first found a few years ago in uranium.[39] They call it 'radioactivity', and even I with my modest science training understand that it will be the greatest breakthrough in human energy production. We can harness endless atomic energy!

"And this is my third piece of evidence that the timeline has changed. In my previous life, radioactivity was not yet discovered in 1899! This is a good change, a very good one. In a decade, we will see smokestacks and chimneys fade away, air restored to its primeval purity. The skies of the 1930s will be clear and wide above the future cities shining with the cleanest energy of all—the pure light emitted by atoms—your atoms, Dalton!"

Dalton sighed. "From what I've seen and heard, my friend, comparing my time to yours, I am still pessimistic. Yes, these decades saw an enormous progress in complicated machinery, but also incredible irresponsibility of the leaders, and the dumbing-down of humanity in general. Why, ancient empires are being restored and cobbled together in the 1860s and 1870s—*Italia*, *Germania*; what an operatic nonsense!"

"One would think that Bonaparte's fate would have taught humanity a lesson—but no," agreed Darwin sadly.

"At least the Corsican only had classical gunpowder at his disposal. Now, to human failings they add profound technical inventions, and the mix could prove to be a deadly one!" said Francis Galton.

"I think humankind is not quite ready for this radioactivity," said Dalton. "Unleashing hidden powers of the atom would be unwise. Please do me a favour," he told Wells, "when you are back in 1899, go to Paris and kindly try to reason with those people—the young Polish lady you mentioned, and those French gentlemen."

"The Time Corps influence is getting stronger," said Wells. "Perhaps we can somehow enforce a halt on atomic research until the first disarmament agreements show up, and the Great Powers will cease their aggressive behaviours. But not yet; not in the 19th century!" He smiled. "My 1899 will end in a few weeks. Our brilliant century is about to be over."

Alice was sitting at her desk at the Crystal Palace.[40] Purchased on the Queen's orders, this magnificent new Royal possession in Sydenham was being rapidly converted into the *Academia Scientiarum Britannica*, to rival any institution of learning of the ancient and modern world—and at the same time to become an official front for the Time Corps's clandestine work.

When completed and refurbished according to plans drawn up by Darwin and Wells, the Palace will house hundreds of resident and visiting scholars from all of the civilized nations, representing all fields of natural sciences and medicine. Incessant trainloads arriving to the station unloaded boxes with specimens, chemicals, books, and equipment. Already a number of men—and women, too—laboured happily along the bookshelves, chemical benches, and dissection desks in brightly lighted halls.

Alice pored over the heaps of charts produced by Francis Galton; his tables on distribution of talent across the world, his coloured space-time maps he drafted to identify hereditary factors associated with various facets of intelligence. Under Mr Galton's supervision, special boarding schools in mathematics and science were now being started by the Time

Corps across England and Scotland. Talented boys and girls, tested rigorously for their inborn intelligence, were brought from all over the globe, from the pampas of South America to frozen reaches of Siberia!

Alice now helped to select the most important maps that were to be photographed on Dodgson's improved glass plates, to be carried across the mists of the River Times to earlier years. The Corps members, starting from the 1820s, clandestinely working under John Dalton, would identify the brightest children of the past, and ensure that their talents would be properly tended to.

Thus, those critical years, as Europe recovered from the madness and aggression of the French terror and Napoleonic conquests, would possibly be used more wisely and less chaotically than they were in the current timeline. And the intellectual potential of the British Empire would exceed anything known by Athens and Rome!

Mr Dodgson, she knew, was now extremely overworked, but in his rare free minutes he laboured on a second book of "Alice's adventures"—this time entirely his own fantasy, set on a chess-board pattern.

Mr Darwin was working on his *Descent of Man*. "Descent into a rabbit-hole?" thought Alice and shivered. The silliness of the ominous *Wonderland* text still bothered her, after all these years.

She picked up the latest attempts of Dodgson and Babbage's work—they still tried to adjust the Analytical Engine, now completed and functional, to decode the *Wonderland* message. Alice did not understand long rows of ones and zeros, which had something to do with how the Engine worked. Lady Lovelace told her it was still anyone's guess—without anything to use as a Rosetta Stone.

Her glance also fell onto pages from Mendel and Dalton's report. They used atomic and molecular theories to decode the structure of pangenetic gemmules. Alice had not yet mastered this part of chemistry—all of that extremely new knowledge, combined and contributed from different scholars along the nineteenth century.

She was looking at strange, short words split into small groups—most were in some kind of code so they presented sheer nonsense. Alice felt, however, that somehow, "somewhen" these words would make all of the sense needed to write an ultimate Book of Life.

Could Babbage's Engine help to make sense out of nonsense? Could Dodgson, with his very keen eye to word games—like his *Doublets*, transforming 'MUD' to 'TAR', or 'RAG' to 'CAT'? Only some combinations made sense in English, such as 'TAG A CAT' or 'GAG A CAT'.[41] Why would one want to tag a cat, thought Alice—and it isn't at all nice to gag cats, especially Cheshire ones.

"Does Mr Galton agree with Mr Dalton?" she muttered, her head nodding. "Or was it Mr Dalton who disagreed with Mr Galton?"

She was tired and getting sleepy. Already huge waves were reaching the shore in her mind; a thunderstorm was gathering above her head. The first gusts of wind blew autumn leaves floating along the silent, dark River Times. She thought she could see a lone time traveller flying through the mists, holding fast to a small, sparkling contraption.

A strange, sinister line from a non-existent poem, which had something to do with a lonesome ship in the cold sea, just floated into her head, another jigsaw puzzle piece of nonsense:

"...for the Snark was a Boojum, you see,"

—and on that cue, trying to understand what this sentence really meant, Alice woke up!

She was still sitting at her desk at Darwin's house in Kent, among dozens of glass jars with the exotic specimens of barnacles still in need of sorting.

Had it all been just a dream? Was she not really involved in a noble and brilliant battle for the better future of human-kind among the most prominent scholars of her time?

Alice sighed, thinking about her many visions, and picked up her calligraphy pen. There will be many labels to write for all the seven seas and beyond, to document a still uncharted natural Wonderland—its space and time, an unending quest.

It was the 21st of September 1866, and less than seven miles away at 47 High Street, Bromley, Mrs Sarah Wells just gave birth to her youngest son.

Notes

CHAPTER I

1 *"his spacious house in Down, Kent"*—Darwin's "Down House" is now a museum and a shrine for any naturalist. Detailed and entertaining biographies on Charles Darwin (1809–1882) are many; see e.g. Johnson, Paul. *Darwin: Portrait of a Genius*. Viking, 2012. The village of Down is now called Downe.

2 *"drowning again and again in a bright well of microscope"*—"Since my years at the Museum of Comparative Zoology in Harvard, I have not touched a microscope, knowing that if I did, I would drown again in its bright well." (Vladimir Nabokov, in: Clarke, G. "Checking in with Vladimir Nabokov", *Esquire*, 84(1), July 1975).

3 *"Mr Dodgson vehemently denies non-Euclidean geometry"*—See Wilson, R. *Lewis Carroll in Numberland: His Fantastical Mathematical Logical Life*. W. W. Norton, 2008. Dodgson even wrote a play, *Euclid and His Modern Rivals* (1879?) where the ghost of Euclid was featured. Dodgson defended Euclid against the modern geometry.

CHAPTER II

4 On *metamorphopsia*, also called *Alice-in-Wonderland syndrome*, see a review by Burstein, S. "The Alice in Wonderland syndrome, an update." *Jabberwocky*, 1994, 23(2): 23–31. Among recent papers, see

Binalsheikh, I. M., Griesemer, D., Wang, S., Alvarez-Altalef, R. "Lyme neuroborreliosis presenting as Alice in Wonderland syndrome." *Pediatric Neurology*, 2012, 46: 185–186; Lanska, J. R., Lanska, D. J. "Alice in Wonderland syndrome: Somesthetic vs visual perceptual disturbance." *Neurology*, 2013, 80: 1262–1264

5 Literature on *hallucinogenic plants and mushrooms* and their pharmacology is endless; see e.g. Letcher, A. *Shroom: A Cultural history of the magic mushroom.* London: Faber and Faber, 2006. On Seer's Sage, see e.g. Zawilska, J. B. & Wojcieszak, J. "*Salvia divinorum*: from Mazatec medicinal and hallucinogenic plant to emerging recreational drug." *Human Psychopharmacology Clinical and Experimental* 2013, 28(5): 403–412.

C H A P T E R   I I I

6 *John Dalton* (1766–1844) who described his own *colour blindness* in 1794, instructed that his eyes should be examined after his death, but the examination revealed that the humours were perfectly clear. In 1995, DNA was extracted from Dalton's preserved eye tissue showing that the famous scholar lacked the middlewave photopigment of the retina; see Hunt, D. M., Dulai, K. S., Bowmaker, J. K. & Mellon, J. D. "The chemistry of John Dalton's color blindness". *Science*, 1995, 267(5200): 984–987.

C H A P T E R   I V

7 *"A gleam—a gleam—from Ida's height"*—Aeschylus, *Agamemnon*, transl. by Edward Bulwer-Litton.

8 *"Hughes machine"*—a printing telegraphic apparatus patented in 1855 by a British-American inventor David Edward Hughes (1831–1900).

9 *"from Moscow to San Francisco, from Shanghai to Mars!"*—see *"From Moscow—to Nagasaki! From New York—to Mars!"*, a famous line from a Russian 'Ego-Futurist' poet Igor Severyanin ("Pineapples in Champagne", 1915)

10 *The Analytical Engine* of Charles Babbage (1791-1871) was never built. Ada Lovelace (1815–1852) is considered the world's first

computer programmer; the programming language Ada was named in her honour.

C H A P T E R   V

11 *"'eerie' state in which a person is conscious of the presence of Fairies... or a form of trance, in which, while conscious of actual surroundings, and apparently asleep, he (i.e. his immaterial essence) migrates to other scenes, in the actual world, or in Fairyland, and is conscious of the presence of Fairies."*—Lewis Carroll, *Sylvie and Bruno Concluded,* Preface.

C H A P T E R   V I

12 *"Poi ch'innalzai un poco più le ciglia"*—

> "When I had lifted up my brows a little,
> The Master I beheld of those who know,
> Sit with his philosophic family.

> All gaze upon him, and all do him honour.
> There I beheld both Socrates and Plato,
> Who nearer him before the others stand."

Dante Alighieri, *Divine Comedy: Inferno,* Canto 4: 131–136 (Transl. by Henry Wadsworth Longfellow, 1867). "The Master of those who know" is Aristotle. His *Metaphysics* opens with the words *"All men by nature desire to know."*

13 *"the book will have 150,000 copies published by 1898!"*—157,000 is an estimate by Clare Imholtz, "Notes on the early printing history of Lewis Carroll's 'Alice' books". *The Book Collector,* 2013, 62(2).

C H A P T E R   V I I

14 *"The mad Queen of Hearts—so unlike motherly Victoria—seemed to her a pure embodiment of a blind and aimless Fury"*—"I pictured to

myself the Queen of Hearts as a sort of embodiment of ungovernable passion—a blind and aimless Fury" (Lewis Carroll, "Alice on the Stage", *The Theatre*, April 1887).

15 *"German patriotic misconceptions... the Englishman turned readily enough toward the vague exaltations of modern imperialism"*—these and some other expressions in this and other chapters are borrowed from H. G. Wells' *The Outline of History*. Doubleday, 1961 (1st Ed. 1920).

16 On Prince Leopold's *haemophilia*, see *e.g.*: Rushton, A.R. "Leopold: the 'bleeder prince' and public knowledge about hemophilia in Victorian Britain." *Journal of the History of Medicine and Allied Sciences*, 2012, 67(3): 457–490.

17 *"the geometry they taught us at school is founded on a misconception, ... there are really four dimensions, three which we call the three planes of space, and a fourth, Time"*—H. G. Wells, *The Time Machine* (1895), Chapter 1.

18 *"geological perturbances as if described by Mr Lyell's pen"*—Sir Charles Lyell (1797–1875), Darwin's friend, was the founder of modern geology. His main work was *Principles of Geology* (1830–33).

19 *"Horror scenario"*—in these words Darwin describes natural selection in his book *On the Origin of Species by Means of Natural Selection; or, The Preservation of Favoured Races in the Struggle for Life* (1859).

20 *"the growing pile of civilization might happen to be only a foolish heaping"*—"He [the Time Traveller]... saw in the growing pile of civilization only a foolish heaping that must inevitably fall back upon and destroy its makers in the end"—Wells, *The Time Machine* (1895), Epilogue.

C H A P T E R   V I I I

21 *"Dodgson's amusing diary of his trip"*—all dated quotations in italics are taken verbatim from Lewis Carroll's "Journal of a tour in Russia in 1867." Pp. 73–121 in: *The Russian Journal and Other Selections from the Works of Lewis Carroll*. Ed. by J. F. McDermott. Dover Books, 1977 (first published 1935).

22 *Samuel Wilberforce, Bishop of Oxford* (1805–1873)—known as "Soapey Sam" in the House of Lords—wasn't universally popular. However, the famous 1860 confrontation (at the same Oxford Museum of Natural History where Alice later studied her barnacles),

between Wilberforce and Thomas Huxley, "Darwin's bulldog", is a part of popular myth, rather blown out of proportion. Wilberforce, in fact, was rather friendly to Darwin—he published a review of *The Origin of Species* that took 17,000 words—and was, in many ways, complimentary! (Johnson, 2012, *op. cit.*).

23 *János Bolyai* (1802–1860), *Nikolai Lobachevsky* (1811–1856) and *Bernhard Riemann* (1826–1866) famously broke through the Euclidean mold into higher dimensions. Bolyai's 14,000-page archive survived because it was seized by the local government. See: Dénes, T. "Real Face of János Bolyai", *Notices of the American Mathematical Society*, 2011, 58(1): 41–51. Riemann's Hypothesis (on the distribution of prime numbers) remains unproven; many of his loose papers were accidentally destroyed after his death, so we will never know how close he came to proving it. Riemann's "hyperspace" concept allowed the later development of general relativity theory, and much of mathematics.

24 *"MUZHIK was supposed to worship and revere his Tsar"*—Wells, *Outline of History*. Wells used the spelling "moujik".

25 *"clay tablets of Nineveh"*—the famous cuneiform Library of Ashurbanipal (7th century BCE) uncovered in 1851 by Sir Austen Henry Layard.

26 *Parchment*, thin, treated hide of animals (calf, sheep, or goat), also *vellum* (the finest kind), contains no plant fiber (cellulose). It was used widely for manuscripts until replaced by cotton-based paper by the end of the 15th century. The skill of parchment-making survives to our time; the Orthodox Jewish tradition prescribes that the holy Torah scrolls be made only of parchment.

27 *"Type Writing Machine"*—Anon., "Type Writing Machine." *Scientific American*, 17(1) (New York). 6 July 1867, p. 3. *"A machine by which it is assumed that a man may print his thoughts twice as fast as he can write them, and with the advantage of the legibility, compactness and neatness of print, has lately been exhibited before the London Society of Arts by the inventor, Mr Pratt, of Alabama.... the laborious and unsatisfactory performance of the pen must sooner or later become obsolete for general purposes... and the weary process of learning penmanship in schools will be reduced to the acquirement of the art of writing one's own signature and playing on the literary piano above described, or rather on its improved successors."*

CHAPTER IX

28 *"Once I saw two beetles and seized one in each hand"*—an anecdote recounted in Darwin's *Autobiography*.

29 *"Pangenesis"*—Our word "gene" is an abbreviation of a "pangene" that comes from Darwin's "pangenesis", a term mentioned in his *The Variation of Animals and Plants under Domestication* (1868). This "provisional hypothesis" assumed the existence of "minute, unseen gemmules", which carry heritable traits.

30 *"In Basel, one Dr Friedrich Miescher"*—Miescher (1844–1895) discovered his *nuclein* in 1869; see Dahm, R. "Friedrich Miescher and the discovery of DNA". *Developmental Biology*, 2005, 278: 274–288. In our timeline, it was not until 1953 that James Watson and Francis Crick at Cambridge decoded the structure of this molecule, known to us as deoxyribonucleic acid, or DNA. See also Schwartz, J. *In Pursuit of the Gene: From Darwin to DNA*. Harvard University Press, 2008.

31 *Count Festetics* in Brünn—a wonderful forgotten story of Count Imre Festetics (pronounced [fɛsˈtɛtitʃ]) (1764–1847), a Hungarian aristocrat and Mendel's predecessor, is told in: Poczai, P., N. Bell & J. Hyvönen. "Imre Festetics and the Sheep Breeders' Society of Moravia: Mendel's forgotten 'research network'", *PLOS Biology*, 2014, 12(1): e1001772.

32 On *Mendel*, see for example Henig, R. M. *The Monk in the Garden. The Lost and Found Genius of Gregor Mendel, the Father of Genetics*. Houghton Mifflin, 2000. Gregor Johann Mendel (1822–1884) indeed visited London in 1862 for the Great Exposition. Darwin never proposed a plausible mechanism of heredity. Darwin's "pangenesis" was revamped by Hugo de Vries who rediscovered Mendel's work in 1900. See Schwartz (*op. cit.*) for more details on these remarkable events in our timeline.

33 *"if it remained uncut in Darwin's library"*—the story of uncut pages of Mendel's 1866 paper in Darwin's library is a commonplace item of scientific lore. Although it is commonly thought that Mendel sent it to Darwin, no copy of "Versuche über Pflanzenhybriden" exists in Down House library. However, the myth is not entirely untrue. Darwin possessed a book, in which "Mendels zahlreiche Kreuzungen (Mendel's numerous crossings)" are noted (as nothing exceptional)—and these pages indeed remain uncut in Darwin's copy. For details,

see: Lorenzano, P. 2011. "What would have happened if Darwin had known Mendel (or Mendel's work)?"*History & Philosophy of the Life Sciences*, 2011, 33: 3–48.

34 *"natural selection will always act very slowly, often only at long intervals of time, and generally on a very few of the inhabitants of the same region at the same time."*—Darwin, *On the Origin of Species*, Chapter 4.

CHAPTER X

35 *The Chronic Argonauts* (1888)—a short story about time travel written by H. G. Wells at age 22.

36 *"I am unaware that time travel was ever depicted in a fictional story,"* said Dodgson. *"Yours should have been the first."*—The Outlandish Watch, which allows one to move back in time up to a month is featured in Lewis Carroll's own *Sylvie and Bruno* written much later (1889): *"What a blessing such a watch would be,"* I thought, *"in real life! To be able to unsay some heedless word—to undo some reckless deed!"* This episode has been cited as "the very first true time-travel story in literature." See: Carter, Lin. "Have Time, Will Travel!" *Fantastic Universe*, 12, January 1960: 98–103. (Clare Imholtz, pers. comm.) However, time travel has been used as a literary device already in Samuel Madden's *Memoirs of the Twentieth* Century (1778). Wells' *The Chronic Argonauts* (1888) was published a year earlier than *Sylvie and Bruno*. An even earlier modern time travel story employing a special watch was Edward Page Mitchell's *The Clock That Went Backward* (1881). Mark Twain's *A Connecticut Yankee in King Arthur's Court* (1889) appeared the same year as *Sylvie and Bruno*.

In Russia, as early as 1824 F. Bulgarin published a fantastic story *Pravdopodobnye nebylitsy, ili Puteshestvie po svetu v XXIX veke* (*'Believable unbelievables, or Travel around the world in the twenty-ninth century'*). Another Russian author Alexander Veltman in 1833 published an utopian novel about the 35th century, *MMMCDXLVIII god: Rukopis' Martyna-Zadeka* (*'The Year 3448: A manuscript by Martin Zadek'*). Later, Veltman wrote *Predki Kalimerosa: Aleksandr Filippovich Makedonskii* (*'The forebears of Kalimeros: Alexander, son of Philip of Macedon'*) (1836) where the hero travels to ancient Greece on a hippogriff.

37 *"Scientific romances"* of H. G. Wells that brought him instant fame were *The Time Machine* (1895), *The Island of Dr Moreau* (1896), *The Invisible Man* (1897), and *The War of the Worlds* (1899).

38 The *First Hague Peace Conference* was proposed on 24 August 1898 by Russian Tsar Nicholas II (1868-1918); it opened 18 May 1899, on the Tsar's birthday.

39 *"amazing properties the French first found"*—In early 1896, Antoine Henri Becquerel discovered radioactivity of uranium. Marie Skłodowska-Curie (1867–1934) and her husband Pierre Curie discovered radium in 1898.

40 *The Crystal Palace* (also briefly mentioned in Ch. 8) of cast iron and glass, built to house the Great Exhibition of 1851 in Hyde Park, was later moved to Sydenham in the south London suburbs. In our timeline, the Crystal Palace burned down in 1936. This iconic symbol of Western civilization and technical progress is reflected in Wells' *The Time Machine* (1895) as the Palace of Green Porcelain of his Year 802,701. It also provides a Utopian vision as seen by Vera Pavlovna Lopukhova in her Fourth Dream in Nikolai Cherny-shevsky's *What is to be Done?* (1863). A pub in Dostoevsky's *Crime and Punishment* (1866) is named "Palais de Cristal" ('Crystal Palace'). Charles Darwin attended the 1851 Great Exhibition, as did 19-year-old Dodgson who was amazed by the Crystal Palace; he wrote to his sister on the 5th of July 1851 that it was "a sort of fairyland".

41 *TAG, CAT and GAG*—some of the *codons* (triplets of nucleotides) in DNA, out of 64 total, that constitute a so-called Genetic Code, discovered in the early 1960s.

Acknowledgements

The author is deeply grateful to his friend, an indefatigable Carrollian veteran, Byron W. Sewell, for a very thorough language editing and addition of several episodes focused on Mr Charles Dodgson, as well as the marvellous illustrations.

Great thanks to Clare Imholtz and August Imholtz, Jr. for reading early versions of the manuscript, and for an endless supply of the Carrolliana!

Leonard J. Deutsch and Michael Everson kindly and thoroughly read the final manuscript.

The author is grateful to his teachers, Raissa Berg, Nina Demurova and Lynn Margulis, for an influence that lasts beyond a lifetime.

The author wishes to thank all his favorite science-fiction authors, especially but not limited to, Poul Anderson, Stephen Baxter, Arthur C. Clarke, Arkady and Boris Strugatsky, and, of course, H. G. Wells. Without them, our future would remain unknown.

Galina Fet's support made this work possible.

This book is dedicated to the 150th anniversary of *Alice's Adventures in Wonderland* and the 150th birthday of H. G. Wells.

SOURCES

Alice's Adventures in Wonderland: The Evertype definitive edition,
by Lewis Carroll, 2016

Alice's Adventures in Wonderland, illus. June Lornie, 2013

Alice's Adventures in Wonderland, illus. Mathew Staunton, 2015

Alice's Adventures in Wonderland, illus. Harry Furniss, 2016

Through the Looking-Glass and What Alice Found There,
by Lewis Carroll 2009

The Nursery "Alice", by Lewis Carroll, 2015

Alice's Adventures under Ground, by Lewis Carroll, 2009

The Hunting of the Snark, by Lewis Carroll, 2010

SEQUELS

A New Alice in the Old Wonderland, by Anna Matlack Richards, 2009

New Adventures of Alice, by John Rae, 2010

Alice Through the Needle's Eye, by Gilbert Adair, 2012

Wonderland Revisited and the Games Alice Played There,
by Keith Sheppard, 2009

Alice and the Boy Who Slew the Jabberwock,
by Allan William Parkes, 2016

SPELLING

Alice's Adventures in Wonderland,
Retold in words of one Syllable by Mrs J. C. Gorham, 2010

𐐉𐑊𐐮𐑅'𐑅 𐐈𐐼𐑂𐐯𐑌𐐲𐑉𐑆 𐐮𐑌 𐐎𐐲𐑌𐐼𐐲𐑉𐑊𐐰𐑌𐐼,
Alice printed in the Deseret Alphabet, 2014

𐐜 𐐏𐐲𐑌𐐻𐐮𐑍 𐐲𐑂 𐑄 𐐝𐑌𐐪𐑉𐐿,
The Hunting of the Snark printed in the Deseret Alphabet, 2016

𐐢𐐳𐐿 𐑄 𐐢𐑀𐐱𐐲𐑌-𐐘𐑊𐐰𐑅 𐐰𐑌𐐼 𐐎𐐱𐐻 𐐪𐑊𐐮𐑅 𐐘𐐱𐑌𐐼 𐐜𐐩𐑉,
Looking-Glass printed in the Deseret Alphabet, 2016

Alice's Adventures in Wonderland,
Alice printed in Dyslexic-Friendly fonts, 2015

∧⌐⌐ꓱ'ꓢ ∧⊃/ꓱ111 ꓴꓤꓱꓢ ɹ11 ∧ ⊃\ �⌐ꓱ∧⌐ ∨⌐11⊃ꓱꓤ⌐∧11⊃,
Alice printed in a font that simulates Dyslexia, 2015

ᚻᛚ⫰ᚻᛚ⫰ᚻᛈᛘ ᚻᛁᚾᛤᚻ⫰ᛚᛁᚻᛚᛁᛘᛘᛘ ᚻᛈᛚ ᚻᛚᛈᛚᚾᛁᛚᛤᚻᛈᛚᛁ,
Alice printed in the Ewellic Alphabet, 2013

'Ælɪsɪz Əd'ventʃəz ɪn 'Wʌndə,lænd,
Alice printed in the International Phonetic Alphabet, 2014

Alis'z Advnĕrz in Wunḏland, *Alice* printed in the Ñspel orthography, 2015

˙ㄴ⸜ㄷ˥ⁿ˥ ˙ꓥ˸ˉ⊓ⁿˮⁿˉ˥ ⸜⊔ ˸⊏⊔⊐ˉ⊓ㄴˮ˙⊔⊐,
Alice printed in the Nyctographic Square Alphabet, 2011

ꓶꟷɼ'ɪꓤ ꞇꞁꞈꞀꝁꞅꝝ ꞁꞁ ˙ꞁꞇꝓꝏꞇꝁ, *Alice* printed in the Shaw Alphabet, 2013

ALISIZ ADVENCƎRZ IN WUNDꓣLAND,
Alice printed in the Unifon Alphabet, 2014

ꟼꝊᚷᚷᚻᚷᚻᚷᚻ ᚷᚷᚷᛏᚷᚷᚷᚷ ᚻᛏᚷᚻ (Aliz kalandjai Csodaországban),
The Hungarian *Alice* printed in Old Hungarian script, tr. Anikó Szilágyi, 2016

SCHOLARSHIP

Reflecting on Alice: A Textual Commentary
on *Through the Looking-Glass*, by Selwyn Goodacre, 2016

Elucidating Alice: A Textual Commentary on *Alice's Adventures in Wonderland*, by Selwyn Goodacre, 2015

Behind the Looking-Glass: Reflections on the Myth
of Lewis Carroll, by Sherry L. Ackerman, 2012

Selections from the Lewis Carroll Collection
of Victoria J. Sewell, compiled by Byron W. Sewell, 2014

SOCIAL COMMENTARY

Clara in Blunderland, by Caroline Lewis, 2010

Lost in Blunderland: The further adventures of Clara,
by Caroline Lewis, 2010

John Bull's Adventures in the Fiscal Wonderland, by Charles Geake, 2010

ALSO AVAILABLE FROM EVERTYPE

The Westminster Alice, by H. H. Munro (Saki), 2010

Alice in Blunderland: An Iridescent Dream,
by John Kendrick Bangs, 2010

SIMULATIONS

Davy and the Goblin, by Charles Edward Carryl, 2010

The Admiral's Caravan, by Charles Edward Carryl, 2010

Gladys in Grammarland, by Audrey Mayhew Allen, 2010

Alice's Adventures in Pictureland, by Florence Adèle Evans, 2011

Folly in Fairyland, by Carolyn Wells, 2016

Rollo in Emblemland, by J. K. Bangs & C. R. Macauley, 2010

Phyllis in Piskie-land, by J. Henry Harris, 2012

Alice in Beeland, by Lillian Elizabeth Roy, 2012

Eileen's Adventures in Wordland, by Zillah K. Macdonald, 2010

Alice and the Time Machine, by Victor Fet, 2016

Алиса и Машина Времени (Alisa i Mashina Vremeni),
Alice and the Time Machine in Russian, tr. Victor Fet, 2016

SEWELLIANA

Sun-hee's Adventures Under the Land of Morning Calm,
by Victoria J. Sewell & Byron W. Sewell, 2016

선희의 조용한 아침의 나라 모험기
(Seonhuiui joyonghan achim-ui nala moheomgi),
Sun-hee in Korean, tr. Miyeong Kang, 2016

Alix's Adventures in Wonderland:
Lewis Carroll's Nightmare, by Byron W. Sewell, 2011

Alopk's Adventures in Goatland, by Byron W. Sewell, 2011

Alice's Bad Hair Day in Wonderland, by Byron W. Sewell, 2012

The Carrollian Tales of Inspector Spectre, by Byron W. Sewell, 2011

The Annotated Alice in Nurseryland, by Byron W. Sewell, 2016

The Haunting of the Snarkasbord, by Alison Tannenbaum,
Byron W. Sewell, Charlie Lovett, & August A. Imholtz, Jr, 2012

Snarkmaster, by Byron W. Sewell, 2012

In the Boojum Forest, by Byron W. Sewell, 2014

Murder by Boojum, by Byron W. Sewell, 2014

Close Encounters of the Snarkian Kind, by Byron W. Sewell, 2016

TRANSLATIONS

Кайкалдыҥ Јеринде Алисала болгон учуралдар
(Kaykaldıñ Cerinde Alisala bolgon uçuraldar),
Alice in Altai, tr. Küler Tepukov, 2016

Alice's Adventures in An Appalachian Wonderland,
Alice in Appalachian English, tr. Byron & Victoria Sewell, 2012

Patimatli ali Alice tu Vãsilia ti Ciudii,
Alice in Aromanian, tr. Mariana Bara, 2015

Алесіны прыгоды ў Цудазем'і (Alesiny pryhody
u Tsudazem'i), *Alice* in Belarusian, tr. Max Ščur, 2016

На тым баку Люстра і што там напаткала Алесю
(Na tym baku Liustra i shto tam napatkala Alesiu),
Looking-Glass in Belarusian, tr. Max Ščur, 2016

Снаркаловы (Snarkalovy),
The Hunting of the Snark in Belarusian, tr. Max Ščur, 2016

Crystal's Adventures in A Cockney Wonderland,
Alice in Cockney Rhyming Slang, tr. Charlie Lovett, 2015

Aventurs Alys in Pow an Anethow,
Alice in Cornish, tr. Nicholas Williams, 2015

Alice's Ventures in Wunderland,
Alice in Cornu-English, tr. Alan M. Kent, 2015

Alices Hændelser i Vidunderlandet, *Alice* in Danish, tr. D.G., Forthcoming

آليس در سرزمين عجايب (Âlis dar Sarzamin-e Ajâyeb),
Alice in Dari, tr. Rahman Arman, 2015

La Aventuroj de Alicio en Mirlando,
Alice in Esperanto, tr. E. L. Kearney (1910), 2009

La Aventuroj de Alico en Mirlando,
Alice in Esperanto, tr. Donald Broadribb, 2012

Trans la Spegulo kaj kion Alico trovis tie,
Looking-Glass in Esperanto, tr. Donald Broadribb, 2012

Les Aventures d'Alice au pays des merveilles,
Alice in French, tr. Henri Bué, 2015

Les Aventures d'Alice au pays des merveilles,
Alice in French, tr. Henri Bué, illus. Mathew Staunton, 2015

Alisanın Gezisi Şaşilacek Yerdä,
Alice in Gagauz, tr. Ilya Karaseni, 2016

ელისის თავგადასავალი საოცრებათა ქვეყანაში
(Elisis t'avgadasavali saoc'rebat'a k'veqanaši),
Alice in Georgian, tr. Giorgi Gokieli, 2016

Alice's Abenteuer im Wunderland,
Alice in German, tr. Antonie Zimmermann, 2010

Die Lissel ehr Erlebnisse im Wunnerland,
Alice in Palantine German, tr. Franz Schlosser, 2013

Der Alice ihre Obmteier im Wunderlaund,
Alice in Viennese German, tr. Hans Werner Sokop, 2012

Balþos Gadedeis Aþalhaidais in Sildaleikalanda,
Alice in Gothic, tr. David Alexander Carlton, 2015

Nā Hana Kupanaha a 'Āleka ma ka 'Āina Kamaha'o,
Alice in Hawaiian, tr. R. Keao NeSmith, 2016

Ma Loko o ke Aniani Kū a me ka Mea i Loa'a iā 'Āleka
ma Laila, *Looking-Glass* in Hawaiian, tr. R. Keao NeSmith, 2016

Aliz kalandjai Csodaországban,
Alice in Hungarian, tr. Anikó Szilágyi, 2013

Eachtra Eibhlíse i dTír na nIontas,
Alice in Irish, tr. Pádraig Ó Cadhla (1922), 2015

Eachtraí Eilíse i dTír na nIontas, *Alice* in Irish, tr. Nicholas Williams, 2007

Lastall den Scáthán agus a bhFuair Eilís Ann Roimpi,
Looking-Glass in Irish, tr. Nicholas Williams, 2009

Le Avventure di Alice nel Paese delle Meraviglie,
Alice in Italian, tr. Teodorico Pietrocòla Rossetti, 2010

Alis Advencha ina Wandalan,
Alice in Jamaican Creole, tr. Tamirand Nnena De Lisser, 2016

L's Aventuthes d'Alice en Êmèrvil'lie,
Alice in Jèrriais, tr. Geraint Williams, 2012

L'Travèrs du Mitheux et chein qu'Alice y démuchit,
Looking-Glass in Jèrriais, tr. Geraint Williams, 2012

Элисәнің ғажайып елдегі басынан кешкендері
(Älīsäniñ ğajayıp eldegi basınan keşkenderi),
Alice in Kazakh, tr. Fatima Moldashova, 2016

Алисаның Кызыктар Өлкөсүндөгү укмуштуу окуялары
(Alisanın Kızıktar Ölkösündögü ukmuştuu okuyaları),
Alice in Kyrgyz, tr. Aida Egemberdieva, 2016

Las Aventuras de Alisia en el Paiz de las Maraviyas,
Alice in Ladino, tr. Avner Perez, 2014

לאס אב׳יבמוראדאס די אליסייה איך איל פאאיס די לאס מאראב׳יליאס
(Las Aventuras de Alisia en el Paiz de las Maraviyas),
Alice in Ladino, tr. Avner Perez, 2016

Alisis pīdzeivuojumi Breinumu zemē,
Alice in Latgalian, tr. Evika Muizniece, 2015

Alicia in Terra Mirabili, *Alice* in Latin, tr. Clive Harcourt Carruthers, 2011

Aliciae per Speculum Trānsitus (Quaeque Ibi Invēnit),
Looking-Glass in Latin, tr. Clive Harcourt Carruthers, Forthcoming

Alisa-ney Aventuras in Divalanda, *Alice* in Lingua de Planeta (Lidepla), tr.
Anastasia Lysenko & Dmitry Ivanov, 2014

La aventuras de Alisia en la pais de mervelias,
Alice in Lingua Franca Nova, tr. Simon Davies, 2012

Alice ehr Eventüürn in't Wunnerland,
Alice in Low German, tr. Reinhard F. Hahn, 2010

Contoyrtyssyn Ealish ayns Cheer ny Yindyssyn,
Alice in Manx, tr. Brian Stowell, 2010

Ko Ngā Takahanga i a Ārihi i Te Ao Miharo,
Alice in Māori, tr. Tom Roa, 2015

Dee Erläwnisse von Alice em Wundalaund,
Alice in Mennonite Low German, tr. Jack Thiessen, 2012

Auanturiou adelis en Bro an Marthou,
Alice in Middle Breton, tr. Herve Le Bihan & Herve Kerrain, Forthcoming

The Aventures of Alys in Wondyr Lond,
Alice in Middle English, tr. Brian S. Lee, 2013

L'Avventure d'Alice 'int' 'o Paese d' 'e Maraveglie,
Alice in Neapolitan, tr. Roberto D'Ajello, 2016

L'Aventuros de Alis in Marvoland, *Alice* in Neo, tr. Ralph Midgley, 2013

Elises Eventyr i Undernes Land: den første norske *Alice:*
Elise's Adventures in the Land of Wonders: the first Norwegian *Alice,*
Alice in Norwegian, ed. & tr. Anne Kristin Lande, 2016

Æðelgyðe Ellendæda on Wundorlande,
Alice in Old English, tr. Peter S. Baker, 2015

La geste d'Aalis el Païs de Merveilles,
Alice in Old French, tr. May Plouzeau, 2016

Alitjilu Palyantja Tjuta Ngura Tjukurmankuntjala (Alitji's Adventures
in Dreamland), *Alice* in Pitjantjatjara, tr. Nancy Sheppard, 2016

Alitji's Adventures in Dreamland: An Aboriginal tale inspired by
Alice's Adventures in Wonderland, adapted by Nancy Sheppard, 2016

Alice Contada aos Mais Pequenos,
The Nursery "Alice" in Portuguese, tr., Rogério Miguel Puga, 2015

Соня въ царствѣ дива (Sonia v tsarstvie diva):
Sonja in a Kingdom of Wonder,
Alice in facsimile of the 1879 first Russian translation, 2013

Охота на Снарка (Okhota na Snarka),
The Hunting of the Snark in Russian, tr. Victor Fet, 2016

Ia Aventures as Alice in Daumsenland,
Alice in Sambahsa, tr. Olivier Simon, 2013

Ocolo id Specule ed Quo Alice Trohv Ter,
Looking-Glass in Sambahsa, tr. Olivier Simon, 2016

'O Tāfaoga a 'Ālise i le Nu'u o Mea Ofoofogia,
Alice in Samoan, tr. Luafata Simanu-Klutz, 2013

Eachdraidh Ealasaid ann an Tìr nan Iongantas,
Alice in Scottish Gaelic, tr. Moray Watson, 2012

Alice's Adventchers in Wunderland,
Alice in Scouse, tr. Marvin R. Sumner, 2015

Mbalango wa Alice eTikweni ra Swihlamariso,
Alice in Shangani, tr. Peniah Mabaso & Steyn Khesani Madlome, 2015

Ahlice's Aveenturs in Wunderlaant,
Alice in Border Scots, tr. Cameron Halfpenny 2015

Alice's Mishanters in e Land o Farlies,
Alice in Caithness Scots, tr. Catherine Byrne 2014

Alice's Adventirs in Wunnerlaun,
Alice in Glaswegian Scots, tr. Thomas Clark, 2014

Ailice's Anters in Ferlielann,
Alice in North-East Scots (Doric), tr. Derrick McClure, 2012

Alice's Adventirs in Wonderlaand,
Alice in Shetland Scots, tr. Laureen Johnson, 2012

Ailice's Àventurs in Wunnerland,
Alice in Southeast Central Scots, tr. Sandy Fleemin, 2011

Ailis's Anterins i the Laun o Ferlies,
Alice in Synthetic Scots, tr. Andrew McCallum, 2013

Alice's Carrànts in Wunnerlan,
Alice in Ulster Scots, tr. Anne Morrison-Smyth, 2013

Alison's Jants in Ferlieland,
Alice in West-Central Scots, tr. James Andrew Begg, 2014

Alice muNyika yeMashiripiti,
Alice in Shona, tr. Shumirai Nyota & Tsitsi Nyoni, 2015

Алисаның қайғаллыг Черинде полған чоруқтары
(Alisanıñ qayğallığ Çerinde polğan çoruqtarı),
Alice in Shor, tr. Liubov' Arbachakova, 2016

Alis bu Cëlmo dac Cojube w dat Tantelat,
Alice in Ṣurayt, tr. Jan Beṯ-Ṣawoce, 2015

Alisi Ndani ya Nchi ya Ajabu, *Alice* in Swahili, tr. Ida Hadjuvayanis, 2015

Alices Äventyr i Sagolandet, *Alice* in Swedish, tr. Emily Nonnen, 2010

'Alisi 'i he Fonua 'o e Fakaofo',
Alice in Tongan, tr. Siutāula Cocker & Telesia Kalavite, 2014

Ventürs jiela Lälid in Stunalän, *Alice* in Volapük, tr. Ralph Midgley, 2016

Lès-avirètes da Alice ô payis dès mèrvèyes,
Alice in Walloon, tr. Jean-Luc Fauconnier, 2012

Anturiaethau Alys yng Ngwlad Hud, *Alice* in Welsh, tr. Selyf Roberts, 2010

I Avventur de Alis ind el Paes di Meravili,
Alice in Western Lombard, tr. GianPietro Gallinelli, 2015

Di Avantures fun Alis in Vunderland,
Alice in Yiddish, tr. Joan Braman, 2015

Alises Avantures in Vunderland,
Alice in Yiddish, tr. Adina Bar-El, Forthcoming

Insumansumane Zika-Alice,
Alice in Zimbabwean Ndebele, tr. Dion Nkomo, 2015

U-Alice Ezweni Lezimanga, *Alice* in Zulu, tr. Bhekinkosi Ntuli, 2014